Small Town Shock

Issy Brooke

Cover credit: background vector illustration Denis
Demidenko via 123rf.com

Cover design and dog illustration by Issy Brooke

2

Author's Hello

Just a quick heads-up on the whole spelling and grammar thing. I'm a British author and this book is set in England. Sometimes, British English looks unfamiliar to readers of other variants of English. It's not just spelling (colour and realise and so on) and not just the vocabulary (pavement for sidewalk, mobile for cell phone) but there are differences even in the way we express ourselves. (In the US, it is more common to say something like "did you see Joanne?" whereas in the UK we would say "have you seen Joanne?" and so on.) Also, my characters do not speak grammatically correct sentences - who does? Not me. Rest assured this book has been copyedited and proofread (errors, alas, are my own and I won't shoot my editor if you find any.)

And another thing - locations. Lincolnshire is real. It's a massive rural county in the east of England, with a sparse population. It's mostly agricultural. Upper Glenfield, the town in this tale, is fictional. Lincoln, the main city nearest to Glenfield, does exist and it's worth a visit. The only thing

I've fictionalised in Lincoln is the layout and situation of the police station.

You can find out more about Lincolnshire and the characters in Glenfield at my website, http://www.issybrooke.com

Why not sign up to my mailing list? You get advance notice of new releases at a special price - but no spam. No one wants spam. Check it out here: http://issybrooke.com/newsletter/

CHAPTER ONE

Though it was May, the air was cool at seven o'clock in the morning, and Penny May wrapped a brand-new bright red scarf around her neck and face. It had been carefully chosen to remind her of the cheerful clothes she used to wear before she was sucked into decades of corporate greyness. It also served to disguise her appearance somewhat, which could only be a good thing. She wanted to be incognito.

She crept to the front door of her recently-purchased cottage, and opened it slightly, just enough for her head to peek out. She looked left and right, and strained her ears. River Street was a dead-end to the left, and all was quiet where the street met the crossroads to the right. Suddenly, a milk float buzzed past. Then, silence once more.

It was safe to leave.

"Come on, you," she muttered, and as she stepped

back to open the door fully, her wildly over-excited dog barged past her, flinging herself into the street with her legs and tail making windmills. Penny was dragged out, and she hauled back as hard as she could to stop the dog in her tracks for long enough that Penny could lock her door. Why was it that the harder Penny pulled, the more the dog would pull back? Contrary animal.

But anyway ... now the door was secure, the mission was on.

Mission "Avoid All Other Dogs".

All dogs.

And possibly men in hats.

And carrier bags.

And invisible things that only the dog could see.

The dog was large, and tall, and broad, and black with tan legs and a tan muzzle. The rescue centre had muttered something about her being a cross-breed but it was obvious to anyone who vaguely knew dogs that she was a Rottweiler.

Sad to say, but when Penny had taken her on, she couldn't even claim to "vaguely" know dogs. But she was on a crash course now.

Penny lurched along behind the dog as she lunged and sniffed her way along the street, moving by stops and starts, heading towards the centre of the small Lincolnshire town of Upper Glenfield.

Penny had only lived in the area for four weeks but she had already established that the town "centre" was a handful of small shops, "rush hour" was when a tractor prevented the fuel tanker getting to the petrol station, and "community spirit" meant that every other dog walker she saw wanted to talk with her.

And that would have been fine.

Except when she'd gone to the animal rescue centre asking for a "friendly" dog, she had not thought to specify that the dog be friendly to other dogs.

She'd owned Kali for a week and she imagined that the whole town already knew her as "that Londoner with the crazy hound." Kali would happily lick anyone to death – the postman included, unless he was wearing a hat – but the minute she saw another creature on four legs, she became a howling, barking, lunging, foaming whirling devil of sheer terror. If she had been a terrier, Penny could have picked her up. But she was not about to snatch a five-stone Rottie up under her arm. Instead, Penny would try to distract her, cajole her, and wrestle her away from the situation. In the one short week of dog ownership, she'd been dragged on her bottom along a grassy bank, leaped behind a pile of rubbish in an alleyway, hidden in some-one's front garden, and squatted between two parked cars while singing lullabies to draw Kali's attention.

Penny dug in her heels and hauled back on Kali as they neared the end of the street. Her heart was pounding as she looked up and down, trying to see around corners and predict what was coming. She wasn't sure what she was most afraid of. It was a mix of fear that Kali would get loose and attack another dog, as she seemed to want to, and also the humiliation that she looked like the worst dog owner in the world.

There was a car pulling into the primary school on her right, and someone walking through the churchyard opposite, but there were no dogs. Hot relief washed along her spine as she turned right and let Kali walk as quickly as she liked, south along Spinney Road and out of the town towards open fields.

* * * *

How had it come to this? Penny asked herself that question a lot. She walked briskly and was soon too warm in her scarf. She pulled it down a little, and inhaled the air – she told herself that the tang of muck-spreading was simply the sweetness of rural life. She walked straight on past a tempting open area to the left. It was called the Slipe, and it was meadow land that bordered the river; apparently

8

"slipe" was a local Lincolnshire word to describe a patch of land that would flood when the river was high. She had never realised that Lincolnshire had an accent, never mind its own dialect, until she moved to the area. It had shades of the rounded vowels of the West Country, with a Yorkshire tinge and some odd Norfolk inflections too. When she overheard older men talking to one another, it sounded like a stream of eee and ooo and aaaa spoken with a mouthful of pebbles.

The Slipe was a popular spot for people to let their dogs run free. Therefore, Penny could not go there, unless she wanted to see carnage and disaster. Instead she had to head for the lesser-used footpaths.

"I was supposed to be here to unwind and leave stress behind," she said to Kali, who had stopped to sniff a particularly interesting patch of grass that looked – but clearly didn't smell – exactly the same as all the other patches of grass beside the road.

Kali's ears swivelled around but she didn't move from her task, her nose buried among the stalks of grass.

"And I wasn't supposed to end up with a dog like you," she added darkly. She'd intended to get something small and cute and happy that would bound along playfully and frolic with other dogs as she watched from a bench. In these fantasies, it was always a warm summer's day and she

9

was inexplicably holding a glass of wine.

She'd need a bottle of the stuff at this rate. Maybe a bottle a day.

Kali suddenly tensed, her head and tail high in the air, her nose wrinkling as some invisible information came to her on the wind. Penny tensed too, and she shortened the lead. She couldn't see any other dogs on the lonely road, but she'd heard that they could smell each other for miles.

Which begged the question quite why they needed to get so close to each other's bottoms when they met.

Kali shook herself and sprang forwards unexpectedly, jerking Penny off balance. She gathered herself, and sighed, following on behind.

* * * *

The road went past a small stand of trees, known locally as the Spinney. A track wound off to the left, called Manor Lane. She could see a smattering of cottages along it, and some large wrought-iron gates at the end, hiding what she assumed was a large house. She hoped an enigmatic and slightly mad Lord lived there. That would be fun.

She continued south. This was a quiet back road, with occasional farm traffic and one or two cars. She wanted to get off the highway, though, and as soon as a path opened up, she took it. She followed it along the edge of a field of unknown crops. Potatoes? Beans? Corn? She had no idea. There was never any sign of life in the arable fields, unlike the picture books of childhood where the farms were brimming with flat-capped men and their plump wives baking cakes. The landscape undulated, rising and falling with gentle hills. She'd thought Lincolnshire was flat but it wasn't. There were some surprising pockets of actual picturesque landscape dotted with an assortment of pretty stone-built farms and huge, industrial barns. She was longing to peep inside one of those vast structures.

The path began to peter out as the gradient increased. She pressed on. She hadn't come this way before, and Kali was eagerly embracing all the new smells. She was following a rough, scrubby hedge along the edge of a field of something short and green and quite leafy. Cabbage, she guessed.

There was definitely no path any longer. This was probably – no, certainly – private land, she thought to herself. I'm going to be shot by an angry farmer, aren't I?

Well, at least I can set the dog on him.

As long as he looks like a dog. Or he is wearing a hat and carrying a bag. Otherwise she'll be no use. She'll run up and make friends and demand treats.

Is this private land?

She could feel her negative thoughts spiralling around her brain again and she sought to stop them. She was here to chill out and calm down, not find new things to worry about. No farmer was going to shoot her, and no pack of dogs was going to spring out of the hedge and attack them, and it might not even be about to rain. She squinted at the low, grey clouds, daring them to try. Once, she had been a wild and confident young woman. She was no longer young, but by goodness she was going to reclaim her youthful fire. It was partly for the sake of her blood pressure, but mostly because … well, increasing age brought increasing clarity, and she had begun to realise that she was working hard simply for the sake of working hard, and one day she would be no more, and what, exactly, had it all been for?

She needed to be the free, happy, wild artist that she had been, so long ago. Hence the red scarf, the new house, the dog, and the strange shade of green that she had painted her fingernails the previous day.

"Bring it on," she said to the world at large.

The gaps in the hedge widened and the crops grew sparse and scrubby at the edges of the field. Now she was walking along a rough ridge, and to her right, the slope was steep as it plummeted downwards. Kali began to pull forwards, hard, and Penny's feet slipped and scrabbled in the mud.

"Wait! Stop! Halt! What word did your previous owners use?" she said though gritted teeth, knowing it was useless. The only commands Kali seemed to know were "sit" and "food" and those meant nothing when she was outside and over-stimulated. Maybe the dog spoke German. It was a German breed. "Sitzen?" she hazarded. For all she knew, that was something terribly rude in German, and didn't mean sit at all. "Achtung?" The only other word she knew was "schnell", from war films, and telling the dog to go faster was not what she wanted to do.

Penny pulled back hard on the lead, but five stone of enthusiastic Rottie was no match for the mud and her flowery, smooth-soled wellington boots, and she hit the ground in a flurry of muffled curses. The lead slipped right out of her grasp and Kali bounded off down the slope, tail held high like a triumphant flag. She almost heard her cry "Freeeeedom!"

"Ugh." Penny sat up, and tipped her head back, closing her eyes for a brief moment. It was Sunday. She should be in bed, reading the newspapers, drinking proper filter coffee, and feeling smug as she planned a lazy weekend of sketching and relaxation.

She shouldn't be feeling mud ooze between her fingers while her idiot dog barked her head off at the bottom

13

of a slope.

Her eyes opened with a snap. What was Kali barking at? She stumbled to her feet and peered through the light mist that coated the valley bottom. She could see Kali as a dark blur at the bottom of the rough hill, her tail swooping from side to side, as she jumped, stiff-legged, back and forth. Her yelps echoed across the empty fields. It wasn't a snarling, "let me rip your face off" bark. It was a series of short, sharp yelps. More a "hey, hey, you, look at this!"

"It's a bag of feed or fertilizer or whatever it is that farmers leave lying around," she said crossly as she half-climbed, half-fell down the slope to reach her dog.

Kali was now frantic with barking, foam forming along her lips as she bounced.

Penny's breath caught in her throat as she got closer. She knew what she could see, now. Her palms went slippery with sweat. She knew it was a body and she didn't want to know that it was a body. Instead she focused on Kali, calling her back with increasing desperation in her voice.

Maybe the man lying sprawled on his back was just stunned. He was next to an electric fence. Maybe he'd wake up in a moment.

Though if Kali's barking hadn't woken him by now…

Feeling sick, Penny reached Kali and grabbed hold of

the lead again. She had to look.

The man was in his late fifties, wearing a dark green set of overalls tied around the middle with orange baler twine, and he had an open-eyed, alarmed expression on his grey face.

He was definitely not just stunned.

Panic rose up in Penny. She dropped the lead again and forced herself to approach, reaching out gingerly to feel for a pulse in his neck. She couldn't run off. She had to do the right thing. "Sir? Sir?" she heard herself jabbering. "Wake up!"

The skin was cold and felt almost rubbery to her touch, and she recoiled, rocking back on her heels in horror, wiping her fingers on her jeans. She pulled out her mobile phone and turned away to make the call she knew she had to make.

* * * *

"It's always the dog walkers, isn't it?" Penny said. She knew she was talking too quickly; she could hear her words tumbling out in a stream as soon as the friendly police woman had led her away by the elbow. She wasn't in uniform; she wore sturdy walking trousers and a quilted jacket in shiny blue. Emergency services swarmed over the area, and a four-wheel drive vehicle was on hand to ferry the personnel to the remote spot. "It's always the dog walkers. I've seen the news. Body found by dog walker, that's what they say. Oh my. I'm going to be a suspect, aren't I? I didn't kill him, you know. Although of course I'd say that. Who was he, anyway?"

The police officer was very short, quite round, and very firm. She smiled. "This way, please, Ms May. Let's go back up to the road. We've got a vehicle there where we can have a little chat."

"Oh no, oh no, a little chat, that's code for..." Stop talking, Penny wailed in her head. I'm driving myself mad, never mind anyone else. She was terrified of what she'd found. She'd touched him. She'd touched him. She tried to wipe her hand on her trouser leg without looking like she was trying to wipe away evidence, somehow.

"Don't worry!" The police woman began to laugh. "I'm not going to bash you over the head for a confession."

"Are you even allowed to say that? There was one time, we were filming in a country in Eastern Europe, my goodness, I don't even think the country exists any more, and we had to ... oh, sorry. Sorry. I am nervous." State the obvious. Way to go, Penny! She would laugh at herself ... in the future.

The police woman shrugged. "I know. It's okay."

They were still at the bottom of the slope and they walked away from the scene, soon picking up a farm track. More police vehicles were arriving and parking up. Kali went ballistic once more, and Penny hung on, but she wanted to throw the lead to the floor and simply cry. Everyone would judge her. It was all too much.

The police woman caught her expression, and said, very calmly, "It's going to be all right. Here. Give me the dog." She held out her hand for the lead.

"She's crazy…"

"Hush, now. Come on." The woman bent and reached into the passenger seat of a police car. Her other hand held onto Kali's lead with a rock-like grip. Kali strained to get away, and then stopped, her senses alert to something new.

Ham. The pink tasty nectar of the god of dogs.

The police woman fumbled with one hand, awkwardly tearing the meat from her sandwiches into tiny squares and flung them to the floor, saying, "Find it. Find, it, girl!" Kali was delighted, and while she was occupied with her nose to the ground, the police woman was able to introduce herself.

"I'm Detective Constable Cath Pritchard. I just need to take some basic details from you, but under the circumstances, I'll ask you to come up to Lincoln police station later on today, when you can, and give a fuller statement there."

"The circumstances being that my dog is uncontrollable?"

"Yes. Well, no, I mean, because you've had a terrible shock and everything." Cath smiled again. "Finding bodies in the fields is not an everyday occurrence around here."

"I'm glad to hear it."

The police woman offered Penny control of her dog again. "If you can take her lead again please, now she's calmer, and I'll make a few notes."

Penny gave her name and address, though she still had to stop and think what her postcode was. "I've only been here a few weeks," she admitted.

"And where were you before?"

"I lived in London. I was a television producer."

The detective constable's neat dark eyebrows rose up. "Oh, really? Ah, that's why you were filming in Europe, then. It all sounds very glamorous. I bet you've met some amazing people. I only meet people in distress. Or drunk. Or dead."

"It was stressful, demanding and tiring," Penny said. "That's why I'm here, in Lincolnshire. It all got a bit much after … too many years." Decades, in fact. She was the wrong side of forty and beginning to feel it. She'd worked hard to achieve what she thought she wanted and once she'd got it … it wasn't enough.

"Are you here on holiday then?" the constable asked.

"No, I've retired."

"You're far too young to retire! I guess I went into the wrong job."

Bless her. "Thanks. It's sort of a retirement but mostly just a change of scene while I work out what I really want." I left it a bit late, she thought. I should have scheduled my mid-life crisis to happen when I had more energy to deal with it.

Cath's eyebrows quivered, but she drew a line in her notebook and didn't pursue the matter. "Okay. And your date of birth, please?"

Penny gritted her teeth and told her, adding, "Yes. I'm forty-five. And single. No emergency contact details, no." She could put her sister, or her parents, she thought. But what use would they be, so far away? It was easier to deal with things on her own.

Cath nodded. "So can you tell me what you were doing out here on private land?"

Ahh. So it was private. Penny looked down at the dog who was apparently licking a stone. She gave the lead a tug. "It's not that I am saying she's a dangerous dog," she said slowly, mindful of the law. "But she's a little, ah, unreliable, when she sees other dogs. And I had no idea how many dogs there were in the world until I ended up with one that doesn't like others."

"She's fine with people, though?"

"She is. She recognises people as walking potential food-dispensers."

"Right. Were you aware you were trespassing, as it happens?"

"No... am I in trouble for that?"

"Only if the landowner presses charges." They fell silent as the body was carried past them, covered discretely. "And I suspect that is highly unlikely."

* * * *

Penny made it back to the cottage with only one further incident. As she had approached the turn for River Street, an elderly man and his terrier had appeared without warning from the churchyard. Penny had taken immediate evasive action, darting behind a large skip that stood out-side the school gates. She had held Kali's collar tightly, peeping over the top of the skip until the man and his dog had disappeared. She hoped no one was watching her. Now she'd be known as "the crazy London woman with the barking dog who goes eating out of skips."

"Come on, you," she said to Kali. "Let's go home."

Back in her cottage, she released Kali and the dog repaid the kindness by barking at a corner of the hallway for about a minute before wandering off to the kitchen for a drink of water.

Now it all seemed very quiet.

She had expected to be inundated with work colleagues and friends from London; they'd all promised to come and visit her new life in the country.

No one had. Few had even kept in contact, and the sporadic one-sided phone calls soon died away. Without the gossip of London life and work to glue the conversations together, it was obvious how little Penny had in common with her old acquaintances.

"I've had more contact with a dead body than my so-called friends of twenty years," she said to Kali as she followed her into the kitchen to make a cup of tea. "Friends? Huh."

But surely it was partly her own fault that she hadn't yet made any new friends. She'd had to creep around with the dog, skulking in shadowy corners, so she wasn't meeting people that way. She didn't go to any clubs or groups. She'd even been shopping in the nearby city of Lincoln rather than visit the local butcher's and greengrocer's places in the town.

Kali cocked her head to one side and looked at her, her brow furrowed. "Yeah, I know how you feel," Penny told her. After her brew she would have to trap Kali in the living room and head up in her car to Lincoln to make her statement to the police.

Then what?

She was here to make big changes in her life, she reminded herself. She had to move on from the shallow city stress that was dragging her down. Reconnect with her careful art student self who had dreamed of rainbows and unicorns. She needed to get rid of her black and grey suits, her kitten heels, her severe hair style, her hour-by-hour plans for her days.

She needed to be free and happy and relaxed and "find herself."

It was a shame that she had found a corpse instead.

CHAPTER TWO

It was only Monday morning and Penny was already exhausted. These were not the relaxing retirement days that she had planned for. At this rate, she'd never get her blood pressure down to a sensible level.

Penny had woken at silly o'clock and taken hyperactive Kali for a quick scoot out of town, although she stuck to the roads this time. It didn't seem like enough exercise for the buoyant dog, but how else could she do it? She looked at Kali's sad face as she pulled her back into the cottage again. Her whole body was saying, "Let's go out again! Let's climb hills and chase rabbits and bark at shadows and have fun all day long!"

"Maybe it would be fairer if I took you back to the rescue centre," she said sadly, unclipping the lead. Was it selfish of Penny to keep her? She had to do the best thing for the dog, regardless of whether she felt as if she had "failed."

Kali froze. She didn't understand words but she could certainly tell if something was wrong. Her eyebrows furrowed and she looked scared.

Penny sighed and rubbed the dog's head. "I'm sorry. I need to learn how to handle you, don't I? They did say you could take a few months to settle in. But will you ever stop trying to attack every other dog that you see? They don't mean you any harm. I promise."

Kali sneezed, licked her own nose, and wiped it on Penny's hand as a gift.

Penny shuddered and straightened up. Maybe there were dog training classes locally. She had no idea what went on in the town – and yesterday's melodrama had convinced her that she needed to get more involved in the community. She didn't even know who the dead man was. At the police station, they'd given his name as a local farmer called David Hart. Cath Pritchard, the kind plainclothes police officer, had mentioned that she lived in the town, too. So Penny knew the names of two local residents

… but one didn't really count any longer, being recently deceased and all that.

Kali gave her another baleful look as Penny left the house. "I'm sorry," she said to the dog, with genuine feeling. Dogs came programmed to cause maximum guilt, apparently. "We'll go out in the car later, maybe. Okay?"

Penny walked down along River Street. The terraced cottages were long and low, built in the local yellow stone, with cramped on-street parking outside. Along the back of the cottages' gardens was an alleyway, which gave all the residents access to sheds and garages. She had a small brick-built outbuilding which held her new – yet old – M21 motorbike. It was a classic, and something she'd lusted after for years. When she'd moved out of London, she'd impulsively bought it; it even had a sidecar, but her dreams of persuading Kali into it had not yet come to fruition. What if Kali saw another dog as they rode along? The image of a Rottweiler launching itself off the back of a motorbike was an alarming one.

At the end of the narrow road, she came to a cross roads. Going right would take her along Church Street, south out of the town past the church and the primary school, over a small bridge and to the Spinney and open farmland. That was her usual dog-walking route.

Left, the road wound through some more modern housing developments with their twisty-turny cul-de-sacs and paper-thin walls. At the northern end of the town was a roundabout with a twenty-four hour fast food place and a petrol station.

Straight on was the High Street which had the shops, the town centre and further along there was the industrial estate. Penny passed the Green Man pub and crossed the road onto the High Street. There was an open area on the right for the weekly market but she had not visited it yet. On the left was a parade of small shops – the post office, a small mini-market food store, a greengrocer that seemed to have twenty different types of potato but no oranges, a butcher with an intimidating display of knives in the window, a florist and a hairdresser. The hairdressing salon had the inevitable bad pun for a name: "Curl Up and Dye."

Under the circumstances, Penny didn't find that very funny.

She'd not experienced much death in her life, which was unusual for someone of her age, she thought. She'd lived a self-contained existence that focused only on work, and the people she met through work, and consequently she'd never grown close enough to anyone to miss them when they went. Her parents were still alive; though elderly, they got on with active lives quite far away. She visited them at Christmas but their social lives left her feeling quite tired as they explained to their daughter that she could only come up and stay at certain times – when they weren't on cruises, they were on walking holidays, or city breaks, or coach tours, or hedge-laying weekends. She suspected they were both bionic now. They'd had that many spare parts replaced and upgraded – hips, hearing aids, eye laser treatment – they were officially cyber-people. They'd last forever.

There was her sister too, of course. And she was only about an hour away. But Ariadne had made her lifestyle choices, and Penny didn't understand them. They had argued so many times, with so many hurtful words. She preferred to push that from her mind. They'd both made the sort of mistakes in their sibling relationship that seemed too difficult to put right, now.

Or too much effort.

Penny stopped at the end of the parade of shops. The road continued past the busy industrial estate, and up to the High School. She didn't fancy running the gauntlet of walking past a gaggle of sullen teenagers so she turned and made her way back to the mini-market.

It was a mini supermarket with all the basics that you needed from day to day. There was a noticeboard in the entrance with various posters and papers pinned to it, which she skimmed past. She browsed along the fruit and vegetables, heading for the bakery aisle at the back.

She knew why they put the bread and milk furthest away. Shops banked on the fact that people came in for the essentials, so they wanted to ensure that the customer passed as many tempting things as possible on the way through to what they actually wanted. By the time Penny reached the bakery section, she had already picked up a chocolate bar and some interesting pesto sauce in a jar, and then forced herself to put them back again.

She was hoping to see if they did freshly baked baguettes but her way was blocked by a woman as wide as she was tall, with the most amazing sixties-inspired hairdo that she'd ever seen. The backcombed black beehive shone with artificial glossiness, and it was teetering on the top of a face that was almost entirely a wide, red smile. The woman had another woman virtually pinned to the racking by her verbal onslaught.

"Dead! Yes! Very dead! But now I do wonder, you know, how his brother is taking it. You know." The beehived woman wiggled her immaculate eyebrows. Her smile was one of the joy of gossiping, not some inappropriate glee at another's demise. Or so Penny hoped. "You know…" the beehive woman repeated. "Eh?"

"Thomas? Oh my. Well, he'd be relieved, I imagine, but you can't really say that, can you?" the other woman said. "Not that I am relieved. God rest his soul and all that. But Thomas…"

"No love lost between them, was there? Now then, that was a bad business. Eh!"

"I was talking about that to my Barney. It strikes me

that he'd probably offed himself. Farmers. There's a high suicide rate with farmers, isn't there? Milk prices. Guns, my Barney said. They have access to guns, you see."

Beehive woman sucked in her cheeks, her smile temporarily fading as a mark of respect to the dead man. "David Hart never did seem like a man who'd take his own life. Too stubborn, eh. What with the paths and his selfishness and that business with them lot. Now, as for that brother of his…"

"Thomas wouldn't commit suicide!"

"No," the beehive woman said, her eyes alight with mischief, "not at all. I mean that Thomas might have done David in! Eh?"

"No! He never would…" her companion said, delighted with the shocking gossip.

Penny browsed along a display of mysterious Lincolnshire plum bread that she had no intention of buying. Was it just bread with plums in? She pretended to study the ingredients. She really wanted to be part of the conversation. Eavesdropping was the next best thing.

"He might of done him in," the beehive woman said.

"People are strange. I seen it on the telly."

"No, surely not. My Barney said that it was suicide. My Barney knows stuff. David had been quite odd lately. I mean, that new woman he was seeing – you know who! – you'd think he'd be happy, even with her, but he wasn't, he was all strange."

Beehive woman tutted. "No woman was ever going to make him happy. That's why he went through so many of them, eh. Or that's what I heard."

"I dunno that he had that many women. No, but my Barney said that he wasn't even going to darts!"

Now it was beehive woman's turn to be shocked. "Not going to darts!" she repeated in horror. "Not. Going. To. Darts! Eh? Eh!"

Penny wondered what was so important about not going to darts. Was it code for something? What nefarious practices was this sleepy Lincolnshire town really hiding? She couldn't hold her tongue any longer. "What's the deal with not going to darts?" she asked, smiling hopefully at beehive woman and her slender companion.

Beehive woman's eyebrows nearly crawled off the top

of her forehead. Her thinner companion answered for her. "His team lost because he wasn't there!" she said with indignation. Both women made eye contact with one another, and flared their nostrils.

Penny felt excluded. She muttered a meaningless acknowledgment, and put the packet of plum bread back on the shelf. The two women had half-turned away to continue their gossip more privately.

After all, it would not be right if just anyone could hear the rumours they were discussing, would it, Penny thought as she gave up on her baguette hunt. She foraged her way along the aisle back towards the till area.

She had decided not to buy anything, so she nodded at the cashier as she sidled past the line of people waiting to pay for their goods. She felt awfully guilty, as she always did, as if she were under some obligation to buy something lest she be thought of as a shoplifter. She stifled the terribly British urge to apologise for her empty hands.

"Were we not able to meet your grocery needs today, madam?"

It was every shopper's worst nightmare. There was a

painfully keen and helpful member of staff, looming out in front of her, sporting the name badge "Warren." He was dressed in a tight beige shirt that did not flatter him; he was a tall, stocky, fleshy sort of man, the type of man who hunches his shoulders to seem less intimidating, but then immediately counteracts that by standing way too close to people.

Penny stepped back.

He moved into the gap she had left.

Ugh. She could smell his shower gel. She said, "Ahh, sorry, I was just browsing. I've just moved here. Just looking." Just repeating just over and over again. Aargh. She felt pinned to the spot by her own politeness.

The man smiled, his pale eyes crinkling at the corners. He wasn't pretending to be happy to help. He really was very, very happy to help. "Welcome to Upper Glenfield!" he boomed. "We're a local shop but we've got all the big-name brands. Everything you could need! Even marmite! Do you like marmite? I'm the store manager. Warren Martin. Call me Warren. And if there's ever anything you think we should stock, do let me know! I'm always here!"

I bet you are. "Thank you. That's good to know." Help. Let me out. No. I loathe marmite. Her gaze slid past the stocky manager to the door behind him.

But he was immobile and blocked her exit, looming over her with a happy smile. "So you're living in Glenfield, then..."

"Yes." She had just told him that, hadn't she? He was smiling in an increasingly unnerving way. She had to fill the expectant silence. "On River Street."

"Lovely cottages, them, I've always thought. I sometimes go down there early in the morning to take photographs. I go there when no one is around. It's the light, you see. Such wonderful morning light."

"Er ... yes." Nothing creepy about that at all, nope, not at all.

His gaze flickered from her face to her left hand and back. Her heart began to sink as his intentions registered in her mind. He took a deep breath and made his move. "Small cottages, too. Not big enough for a family... on your own, are you? So, if I might ask, if I might be so bold, ahahaha, what brings you to Glenfield?"

She wondered, briefly, if she ought to meet his expectations. She could spin a heart-rending tale of failed love affairs, maybe a marriage break-up, how she was fleeing some dreadful past and was looking only for a new shoulder to cry upon … his wolfish look was certainly hoping for all that.

"I've retired," she said, sharply, and stepped to one side. She was being rude by walking away but then, she reasoned, he was being rude in preventing her from moving on.

"Goodness me. You're far too young to retire," he oozed. "Now then. I wonder if I might be allowed to help you to settle into the area? I've been a long standing resident for many years. I know everyone. I am sure I can help you to get to know people…"

It was exactly what she wanted. But not from this over-keen man who was looking at her with more than friendliness on his face. She said, "What a lovely offer. Thank you but—"

"Perhaps a meal?"

She tried not to groan. "Oh, no, I…"

"Lincoln is not far away. Have you been? Such an overlooked city. It has some wonderful places to eat. The Bailgate area is particularly sophisticated. I know a smashing pub. Tonight, perhaps? Yes! I am free from … well, I shall get Colin to cover for me, so anytime from eight …"

She shook her head decisively. How had "let me tell you about Glenfield" become "let's go on a date in a nearby city"?

"Thank you, Warren, but no thank you. I must be going." She strode past him. These situations needed to be clear and unequivocal. She'd learned that the hard way, some years ago. There had been a pleasant, if slightly drippy, sound electrician on her production team when they were in Cambodia and she had been too soft to give him the brush-off properly. This meant he had followed her around hopefully for four months once they returned to the UK and she had taken to hiding in cupboards just to avoid him. She'd been caught by a security guard who had days of footage of her shenanigans, and she had a lot of explaining to do.

It was far less cruel, in the long term, to simply say

"no."

But Warren was undeterred. She began to recognise him as one of those men who had been turned down so many times that he no longer really registered a proper, clear refusal. He followed her out of the shop and onto the pavement, saying, "It's a simple neighbourly offer, that's all. I'll show you the sights, tell you who is who and what is what…"

"No, but thank you."

He was quite ugly when he was annoyed. "You needn't act like I've just propositioned you. I'm making a friendly gesture."

"And I appreciate it," she said tightly.

"You don't seem to."

She backed away, wishing for the first time that she had her dog with her. Kali could at least look menacing. "I am settling in very well, and I like living here, and I appreciate your offer but now I need to go. Good day." She added "leave me alone" in her head, and hoped he could read that through the narrowing of her eyes.

"You women are all so …"

She turned and walked briskly away, not needing to hang around to hear what he thought of all women. It's a self-fulfilling prophecy in a way, my friend, she thought. You come on too strong and we run away and then you get angry and try even harder the next time … it's never going to work.

It was a shame.

And she had the prickling feeling along her spine that he was staring at her as she went, and she wondered how much of an enemy she had made.

Enemies were easy enough to handle in London. She'd made a few, after all. But here in Glenfield, she was going to find it difficult if people started to take against her before she really got established.

Warren would probably turn out to be a local mover-and-shaker with influence in every corner of the town. She shuddered and headed for home.

CHAPTER THREE

But her cottage on River Street didn't feel like home quite yet. She'd lived in a small apartment in London, so she had been able to bring most of her belongings with her, but even with her familiar items around, it was an unfamiliar sort of place.

Kali was lying in the hallway, doing a fine impression of a large black rug, but she kept her eyes on Penny in case she suddenly decided to shower food everywhere. Dogs were ever-hopeful.

Penny prowled from room to room. It didn't take long. The cottage's front door opened into a tiny porch where she kept boots and coats and hats, and then that opened into the long, narrow hallway. To the right was the main living room at the front of the house, and further down the hall was the square kitchen. Bizarrely, the stairs to the two bedrooms and tiny bathroom led up from a corner of the kitchen.

"I am going to put some pictures up," she told the dog, who cocked her head. "Don't freak out when I start bashing into the walls with a hammer, okay?"

Kali didn't. She followed Penny into the living room and watched as she began to put some nails into the walls. How could the dog go crazy when it caught a glimpse of another dog half a mile away, and ignore this racket? She was learning more about dogs. Ever-hopeful … and they made no sense.

Penny pushed it from her mind. She was hanging a picture from many years ago. She'd painted it herself, in watercolours. It showed a mountain ridge with a cloudy sunset behind it, and it was one of the first paintings that she'd been so pleased with that she had had it professionally framed.

She stepped back and considered it. Yes, she still liked it. It was calm but the mountain had an air of potential menace; in the winter it would be deadly.

She remembered the art student she had been. She'd been lively and yet relaxed, curious and confident, eager to grab life and run with it. Of course, younger folk never really thought they'd ever get old and that time would run out. She'd fallen into the television production world through the design side of things, proved herself a good and capable organiser, and somehow ... somehow her career had taken over, and she had pursued it, thinking that's what she had wanted all along.

But when she'd achieved everything, the status and the money and the swanky flat in central London and the car – and the overpriced parking space to go with it – she felt oddly bereft. Now what?

She was startled from her reverie by the ringing of her phone and she darted through to the kitchen to fumble around in her bag. She retrieved it while it was still ringing but shoved it to her ear before she really registered who was calling.

"Hey, Penelope. How's country life?"

Francine? What was Francine Black doing, calling her? Penny had hoped she'd been left behind in London. Francine was the one of the few people Penny hadn't given her phone number to. The ditzy woman meant well, but goodness, she seemed to see the world as a place of brightly coloured flowers and fluffy kittens. Penny couldn't help but say, quite bluntly, "Oh. What do you want, Francine?"

"I couldn't wait to hear from you! How are you doing? Oh my gosh, it's all so exciting! Leaving the rat race, wow. I'm so pleased for you. What is your cottage like?"

Penny rolled her eyes at Francine's stream of childlike enthusiasm. She had been a rival television producer and they had sometimes worked together and sometimes in opposition. While Penny had embraced corporate life and culture with studied seriousness, Francine had blithely drifted through her career, giggling and bouncing and being everyone's friend. And somehow, it hadn't done her any harm. She was the least professional person Penny knew.

Maybe, Penny acknowledged, she resented Francine's natural exuberance.

But good heavens, the woman was like an over-excited teenage girl with a new set of sparkly shoes. Pink ones, obviously.

Penny leaned on the small kitchen table and gazed out of the window, the phone clamped to her ear. "My cottage is small and sweet and quiet. Er, so how did you get my number?"

Francine tutted and laughed with delight. "Bob Channings who was dating that ferocious Liza woman, no, wait, Lisa, Liselle, I can't remember. The one with the ears."

"Everyone has ears."

"No. The ears. Different sizes. Once you saw it, you couldn't unsee it."

"Lisbeth," Penny said with a sigh. Oh yes. Those ears.

"Yes, Lisbeth! She had your number. I knew you'd moved. Leicestershire, is it? Nice cheese. Have you had the cheese?"

"Lincolnshire. They have bread with plums in, and some strange ham with bits in called haslet, and sausages … also with bits in. Basically, Lincolnshire food is normal food but with extra bits in it."

"It sounds yummy!" said Francine. In a more serious voice, she said, "But who on earth moves to Lincolnshire? It's the sort of place you come from, not go to."

"That's exactly why I'm here. So people don't bother me," Penny added pointedly.

"What are you doing with your time? Have you joined

masses of clubs? Are you bored? Have you learned to knit?"

Penny thought if she rolled her eyes much more, they'd roll right out. "No, I am not bored. I have a dog and a cottage and I'm getting involved with local activities…"

"Such as? Women's Institute, that sort of thing? You, making jam, how wonderful. I'd love to make jam. I tried once but it stayed runny."

"There are shops here. There's no need to make jam. And there's lots to do. Yesterday I found a dead body."

That stopped the conversation in its tracks. Penny smiled to herself. You weren't expecting that, were you?

Francine cleared her throat and said, "Are you joking? It's a sick kind of joke."

Penny felt guilty. Poor bubbly Francine. Why did happy people bring out the worst in Penny's nature? "I'm sorry. No, I'm not joking. I found a dead man out in the fields. I called the police and everything." She was about to ramble on, but she stopped herself. Suddenly, Penny was struck by the lack of people she could talk to. She wanted to spill the details she'd heard about the poor man, and his brother, and how he hadn't been to darts and that must mean something… but she couldn't say all that, not to

44

Francine. Francine was so keen and eager to be her friend and somehow, it just put Penny off.

But it was nice to talk to someone from her past. She had to acknowledge that.

"Are you all right?" Francine asked with genuine concern at the news and the sudden silence.

"Yes, yes, of course I am." Penny was surprised and slightly embarrassed to hear a catch in her voice. She cleared her throat and repeated it. "I am fine. I coped."

"You always cope with everything!" Francine said in admiration. "I wish I was like you. I don't cope. I have a big blow-up with stress, and then carry on."

Maybe that was the way, Penny thought. She was about to answer when she heard Kali erupting into barks from the other side of the house. She could hear Francine asking about the noise, and she made her hasty excuses to finish the phone call.

"Thank you for calling … I really have to go … the dog, you know…"

I should have asked her about her life, her job, her mood, Penny thought as she went to find out why Kali was so upset. It turned out to be a moth battering itself against the window. Penny rescued it carefully and let it fly free in the back garden. Then she stood at the back door, leaning against the frame, looking at the rapidly growing grass. Kali came out to sniff the bare flower borders.

Now she'd shaken Francine off, she illogically wanted to talk to her again.

I must be going daft, she thought. I never wanted to talk to her in London. She was too loud and silly and flippant.

Too much like the person I once was … that I want to recapture.

I'm jealous.

* * * *

The call from Francine would have upset her equilibrium except Penny had to acknowledge that she had precious little equilibrium to start with. When it got to five o'clock she decided to take the dog out for a walk again. She had soon learned, moving out of the city, that in this rural area, the evening meal was eaten earlier than London, and it wasn't called dinner. No, five o'clock was teatime.

Sometimes it was six, depending on where family members worked. But things certainly seemed quieter on the pavements, even if the roads were busy, and she wanted to see if it would be a better time to walk Kali.

She snapped on the lead and gave the dog a pep talk in the hallway before leaving. She knelt down and stroked Kali's shoulders. "You must behave," she told her. Kali hung her head. "You need lots of exercise. How can I give that to you, if you lunge after every dog, barking like a monster? It's no good. I don't want to look like a terrible dog owner. So are you going to behave?"

Kali licked her lips and turned her head away. Penny narrowed her eyes. Dogs couldn't feel guilty, so what was she trying to tell her?

I need to find a library and learn some dog body language, she decided. She stood up and peered out of the front door. It was cloudy and overcast. It was daft, but she welcomed bad weather. It made it far less likely that she would encounter other dogs and their owners.

"We had better get this sorted by the summer," she said to Kali as they left the cottage and walked briskly along River Street. She turned right, heading south again. She felt restricted in where she could go, but it was too risky to turn left and go through town to find the footpaths on that side of the settlement. It would take too long, exposing her to too many potentially unexpected dogs. So, south it was.

They went past the Spinney and continued to follow the road. On her left were the farmlands that she had trespassed on, where she had found the dead farmer. She couldn't help wonder how he had died. It was a funny place to commit suicide, and how had he done it? There had been no gun near him.

Kali was keen to be out and she felt a pang of guilt that she wasn't letting her run off-lead. But she hadn't had her long enough to have built a proper bond, and she had no idea if Kali would come back if she called her. And though she regretted taking the dog on, she didn't really want her running off and never coming back.

They walked on, until she came to a path that left the road and wandered along a field margin. It was marked with a green sign, so she followed it, and slackened the lead so that Kali could ferret about in the hedge to her heart's content.

The path was well-trodden and she began to feel

nervous as it disappeared around a stand of trees up ahead. Her palms were clammy and her head began to feel like it was in a tight vice as she imagined thirty-two dogs appearing and charging at them, and Kali ripping them all to bits, and Penny ending up in jail for lack of control, and dying alone in a cell.

Her heart was thudding and she realised she had stopped walking. Kali was staring up at her in concern.

"On my gosh, I am so sorry," she said in a rush to the dog. She shook her head and closed her eyes for a moment, repeating some calming mantras to herself. She'd been sent on a business-related "de-stress" event once, and now she was making use of the very things she'd once laughed at. "I am calm. I am an ocean of light and peace. Good energy in" –she breathed in deeply– "and bad energy out."

And this worked well until a male voice startled her, making her shriek and choke. "Now then. Are you all right? Meditating or something?"

Her eyes flew open. She still wasn't used to the way the local people used "now then" as a way of greeting, and she certainly wasn't used to tall, sandy-haired strangers appearing on lonely footpaths while she was fighting off what felt like a panic attack.

"I! Oh! Yes!" she blurted like she had landed from an alien spacecraft. "No!"

"Good evening to yourself, too," the man said. "What a lovely looking dog. Is she a Rottie?"

"Yes. The rescue centre had said crossbreed," she added, giving Kali a hard stare, as if she had been in disguise. "I think they thought it would be harder to rehome her if they admitted she was actually a Rottweiler."

"What a beauty. Can I say hi to her?" The strange man kept his distance while he spoke, letting his gnarled hands hang by his sides. She noticed that although he was complimenting her dog, he wasn't looking at the dog directly, which she thought was strange. He was dressed in faded jeans and a fisherman's jumper that was threadbare in places and hairy in others. It had seen better days. Possibly in the previous century.

"She seems to like people," Penny said. "In that, she lunges towards them, wagging her tail."

"Tail wags aren't always a good thing," the man said. He turned to one side and cocked her head, glancing at the dog and then looking away. He yawned. How rude, Penny thought.

Kali looked at him, then up at Penny. Penny's stomach lurched. Was the dog asking for permission?

Or reassurance?

"Go on, then." She nodded at the man. "Say hello."

Kali walked forward and sniffed at his feet, and then his legs. After a few seconds, he patted the side of her neck very briefly, then stopped. Kali leaned against him for more, so he patted her again. "There's a beautiful girl. What's her name?"

"Kali. And I'm Penny. I've just moved into a cottage in the town."

"Hi, Penny. I'll not shake your hand – forgive me – I'm a bit grubby." He showed her his dark-stained palms. His hands were wide and his knuckles very knobbly. "I'm a blacksmith, mostly, with other stuff, you know. Sorry, names, ahh. I'm Drew."

She liked his broad grin, and said, brightly, "Hi, Drew. It's lovely to meet you." Lovely to meet someone who isn't creepy or dead, in fact. "So, tell me, where does this path lead to?"

He turned and waved towards the trees. "Around

there it splits into two, but you wouldn't want to take the left hand path. It leads up to Farmer Hart's land and he's a … he was a stickler for the old 'get orf my land' stuff. He, ahh, sadly he's just…"

"Yes, I know. I found the body, actually." She heard a strange tone in her voice. Was that pride or something? How awful. She tried to compose her face into something serious and respectful.

"You did? It was you? I heard talk. So you're that woman from London. Oh. That must have been traumatic."

"It was strange. I think it would have been worse if I had known him, you know?" She had to add, after a moment's pause, "And what do you mean, 'that woman'? It sounds a little … ominous."

Drew simply grinned more widely. "Welcome to a small town. We know everything about you already. You were taking a risk being on his land, you know. Well, obviously you didn't know."

"I might be a soft London type but I am pretty sure you can't just randomly shoot people anymore."

"No, but you can shoot dogs if they might worry the

sheep. They don't even have to be attacking. The dogs, I mean. Not the sheep. Not that many trained attack sheep around here. Anyway. David Hart got rid of his sheep a few years back and went over to arable. Still, he's put up electric fences absolutely everywhere."

"I did wonder about that." Penny looked over the fields. "It's all crops, so why does he need electric fences? How dangerous can carrots get?"

"That's broccoli in there, or it was," Drew corrected her. "But it's all harvested now. Heh, it can be vicious stuff … I never touch it, myself. But you're right. He doesn't have … didn't have … any livestock at all any more. No, the electric fences were to annoy the local ramblers' club."

"Really?" Penny was immediately intrigued.

Drew nodded. "Yeah. He was really possessive about his land. There was an ongoing thing about a footpath that the ramblers said was a public right of way, because it had been used for a certain length of time so it had passed into common usage or something, and was marked on an old map, and he disagreed. Flatly refused. I don't know what harm it would have been, but anyway. In the ramblers' group, there was one guy, Ed whats-his-face, who was trying to take it to court and everything."

"Did he have support? The ramblers, I mean?"

"From some people, yes. But Ed's pretty new to the area and some people think he's a bit ... of a hippy."

"How long does someone have to live here to be considered local?" she asked. "I need to know…"

"Oh, only two or three ... generations."

"Great." She rolled her eyes at him and he laughed. "I suppose you and your family have lived here since the Norman Conquest."

"Are you kidding?" he said. "We're still bitter about it."

A fat blob of rain fell and she shook her head, looking up. "I guess I ought to be getting back. It was nice to meet you, Drew." Certainly nicer than meeting Warren, she thought. Way nicer.

"I'm walking back to town. May I walk with you?"

"If I say no, it's going to be really awkward."

"No, it's fine," he said, laughing as he fell into step alongside her. "I'll keep a discreet distance behind you."

"Like a stalker."

"Uh, yeah, okay. That will look weird. I'll have to walk

beside you, then. Sorry."

"I'll suffer it this once."

"Thanks."

They soon reached the road. The rain was a light drizzle now. Drew laughingly called it a "mizzle" – apparently a mixture of mist and drizzle. When they got onto the pavement by the road, Kali decided she'd been on her best behaviour for long enough, and lurched without warning down a ditch, heading straight to some temptingly brackish water at the bottom.

"Get back up here!" Penny was dragged behind, trying not to lose her grip on the lead, with her feet scrabbling ineffectively for purchase in the treacherous mud. "Kali! No!"

Kali reached the bottom of the ditch and happily bounded along for a few steps before deciding that she didn't like the feeling of her paws in mud, after all, and she tore back up to the pavement again. Penny felt hot with shame as she scrambled up. "I am so sorry," she muttered. "I'm new to dogs, and … ugh. Just, ugh."

"Don't apologise! Are you all right?" Drew's hands hovered, as if he wanted to reach out and help. He dithered, and shoved them back into his pockets.

"Yeah, I'm fine. Dented pride, that's all." Penny hauled on the lead to get Kali closer. "She doesn't listen to me but I am going to find some training classes. I've got to."

"How long have you had her?"

"About a week."

Drew smiled. They moved off again, Penny keeping Kali at her side. Her shoulders ached with the effort. Drew said, "It's early days, yet. But she looks strong. It's that Rottie muscle around her neck and shoulders. I don't think that collar and lead is the best thing, you know."

"Some bloke I met said I should get a choke chain," she admitted. That bloke had been a horrified man who'd been waiting for a bus, minding his own business, and who had witnessed Kali leap at a passing terrier, apparently intent on murder. She had resented his unsolicited advice.

Drew shook his head. "You haven't, so I am guessing you don't like them."

"No, I don't. It doesn't seem right to strangle the poor thing. But the way it's going, maybe I'll have to try it."

"No, don't," Drew said very firmly. "Not the choke

56

chain. There's always another way. Watch her reactions. You need to bond with her, but take it slow. It will happen."

"I'll keep trying." They reached the crossroads in town. "Here's my street." She wanted to ask where he lived, but her tongue seemed to dry up.

He nodded, and rubbed Kali on the head. "Get in and out of the rain. Don't worry about your dog. I'm sure she'll settle. Take care, now."

"And you." She tugged on the lead and walked away. She was acutely aware of the large brown stain of mud that was inevitably spread across her bottom. Her hair would be everywhere, and she'd be a general mess.

Not that it mattered or that she was in any way concerned, of course.

Not at all.

Kali rolled her eyes up at her, mouth partly open as if she was laughing at Penny. Penny frowned. Kali dropped her head and scurried on.

She thought about the dead man, David Hart. So, it wasn't just the farmer's brother who might have taken against him, she said to herself as she let herself in to the cottage and Kali shot down the hallway before Penny could grab a towel for her paws. In the enclosed space, the pungent smell of wet dog was immediately apparent. She paused, thinking. The local ramblers had issues with the farmer, too.

If it wasn't suicide – though she still thought it could be – then it might have been an accident… but what if it was murder?

I'll follow this story, she said to herself. I'll start buying the local paper and learn who is who. It will give me something to talk about, and I can become a part of this community. Shared experience, and all that. After all, as I found him, I can contribute to the … to the, er, gossip.

There was a crash from the kitchen, and Penny sighed. "Kali!"

CHAPTER FOUR

Penny walked Kali early on Tuesday morning and then spent a fruitless few hours on the mobile phone trying to organise getting broadband internet sorted to her cottage. The previous owner hadn't had a landline and Penny was appalled to learn of the connection charges she was going to incur. Didn't these companies want her business? She was desperate to get online so she could learn a little more about the community, and also about dog training.

I suppose I'll have to pretend it's like 1990 or something, she thought, sitting glumly in the living room with a half-eaten sandwich in her hand. Back when we had to learn things by observation and thinking, not just googling. Huh. When I was a student, it seemed easy. But I suppose I didn't know what I was missing.

She was still trying to reconnect with her light and happy mid-twenties self. She was doing this by listening to the music she had loved, and dressing in bright, cheerful colours. Currently, some strange electronica was wafting out of her iPod docking station and her stripy socks were irritating her calves. Had the music really been this bad back then?

Kali stared fixedly at the sandwich which was limping hanging from Penny's fingers. The dog's unceasing glare started to unsettle Penny so much that she didn't want to eat the rest of it. She stood up and went to the kitchen, and half-heartedly did some cleaning up.

It was no good. She had to get active and involved. She shook herself all over, just like Kali did, and ferried herself out to the mini-market once more. She remembered they had a noticeboard of local events and groups. It seemed like a good place to start.

* * * *

It was still overcast but the rain had eased overnight. She was fed up of the long, drawn-out chilly spring now, and longed for summer to make its appearance. She buttoned up her jacket as she approached the food store. Partly it was against the cold, and partly because she remembered her meeting with Warren and she wanted some kind of armour against his advances. No doubt he tried it on with every new woman who came into the shop; she didn't flatter herself to think that his advances were directed to her alone.

The gossipers had mentioned that David Hart had possibly had a string of women, too. Was that true, or was it sour grapes on the part of the beehive woman? Certainly, she never believed gossip about other women's love lives as it was invariably untrue. Though perhaps he really had been more successful in his affairs than Warren was. She could only see the farmer's lifeless face in her imagination, and it wasn't one that screamed devilish attraction, though.

The noticeboard was by the entrance and she kept alert to the potential approach of Warren as she began to scan the posters. Upper Glenfield Camera Club. Craft Group. Over-Fifties Aerobics. Gemstones for Beginners with Reginald Artichoke. Was that a person or a pop group, she wondered.

A short, stocky woman was pinning something up and it was only when she turned around that Penny recognised Cath Pritchard, the detective constable who'd first interviewed her.

"Now then! Hi, Penny, how are you?" She was dressed in a comfortable looking long skirt and a fleece jacket that had gone bobbly with wear. She was straightening her poster which appeared to be advertising some kind of kitchenware party. Did such a thing exist? Penny wasn't even sure. Foam parties, yes. Dinner parties, okay. Kitchenware? "I hope your gruesome discovery hasn't put you off living here," Cath added, stepping back to assess her poster's placement.

"No, not at all," Penny said. "I'm settling in well. Can I ask … if it's all right, I don't know … how did he die? I overheard people talking about suicide and all sorts of things."

"Huh, small town gossip," Cath said, shaking her head in disapproval. "People round here with nothing better to do. Don't listen to them. I can tell you how he died, though. It will be in the paper at the end of the week, so it's no big secret. Believe it or not, he was electrocuted."

"Really! I didn't think you could be electrocuted to death by an electric fence. Goodness. I'll take more care when I'm out and about. Perhaps it was an accident? It could have malfunctioned."

Cath shook her head again, grim-faced. "The shock throws you clear. Well, not quite the shock itself." She grimaced. "I've been learning a lot about electrocution. Apparently your muscles all go stiff and that's what throws you across the ground. There isn't anything magic in the electricity itself."

"But there isn't enough power in an electric fence, surely? Even to make your muscles go all stiff. Don't people pee on them for a dare? Unless he'd rigged it up to the mains. Do they run off the main grid? And he didn't like the ramblers, did he?" She stopped herself. She could hear her own voice ranting on. So, this is what happened when you stopped working. With fewer people to talk to, all the words bottled up and poured out in a flood when they got a chance.

Cath pressed the final pin into the poster and stepped back. "There's definitely not enough power in the fence. It ran off a battery pack, they say. Some fences are wired to the mains, and some aren't. It's an odd situation."

"Could someone have made him hold on to it?" The farmer was killed by electricity. He was next to an electric fence. It was obviously connected. "In fact, if you were determined to kill yourself, and had run out of paracetamol or gin or whatever, you could just hang on, couldn't you? Unless the muscle thing is involuntary. Yes. Or could it have been tampered with, that battery pack? Super-charged? You have checked, haven't you?"

"The scene of crime team will be all over it. Our clever techy boffin types are wildly excited," Cath said. "They will work it out. But I doubt that you could hang on to a fence until it shocked you dead, no."

Penny's mind was running overtime. It sounded unlikely to have been suicide. The fence had to have been tampered with. There was so much she didn't know about electric fences, she thought in frustration. I need the internet in my cottage! She was about to ask Cath if there was anywhere with internet access in the town, when she spied Warren lingering by the magazines a few feet away. As soon as she caught his eye, he turned towards them and bore down on them both.

She couldn't let Cath leave now – it would abandon her to the clammy hands of Warren. "So, you're running a kitchenware party!" Penny said brightly, clutching at straws. Cath was already turning to go. Penny wanted to look like she was deep in conversation and she walked alongside Cath as she made for the exit.

"It's just a little hobby to bring in extra cash for Christmas," Cath said. "And it's nice to do something completely unrelated to my day job, and feel like a normal person for a while. It's being held tomorrow night at my house. I had a poster up for a while but it got lost. Well, I say 'lost'. Certain groups in the town are not afraid to take other people's posters down." She sniffed. "The Camera Club are particularly underhand. Anyway, do you fancy it? My party, I mean. It would be a great way for you to meet people!"

It would, but it sounded dire. "What happens at this sort of party?" Penny asked. "I went to one in London once. Except it wasn't for kitchenware. It was more … adult. And it was hugely embarrassing and I swore to never go to one again. I bought some furry handcuffs and then got very drunk to blot it all out. I rode home in a taxi and when I woke up, I had 'Ginger Rogers' written in marker pen on my forehead. I still don't know why."

"Oh dear. I know the sort of thing you mean. I think my husband would laugh his face off if I ran a party like that. But I've got two kids and it's bad enough keeping them out of the way when we're all discussing plastic storage boxes, never mind … all that other stuff. No, it's just a bunch of women who come and look at handy things for the kitchen and you can buy things if you like. There will be nibbles. No marker pens. Go on. Do come."

"Ladies, if I may…" Warren said behind them, catching them up.

Penny walked faster, swishing though the automatic doors and Cath kept pace. "I'd love to come," Penny gabbled. "You'll have to give me your address."

"Of course." By unspoken mutual consent they darted across the road to the covered market hall.

"He can't leave the shop while he's working, can he?" Penny asked, not daring to look back.

"I don't think he leaves it even when he's not working," Cath replied. "It's like a self-imposed restraining order." They sidled into the wide entrance of the market.

Penny peeked in the direction they'd come. Warren was in the window of the mini-market but someone was trying to attract his attention with a frozen leg of lamb, and he had to turn away. "We're safe," Penny said.

Cath was already writing her address and phone number on a piece of paper torn from a police officer's pocket book. Penny wasn't sure that she really wanted to go to a party that involved the discussion and sale of plastic tubs; it didn't sound wild enough to be called a "party." But it would be a good way to meet folks, she had to agree, and Cath seemed to think it was a done deal. And she owed Cath for letting her escape Warren with her.

Cath handed her the paper. "So you met Warren before, have you?"

"The other day." Penny shuddered.

"Did he ask you out?"

"He did. I guessed he tries to ask every woman out."

"Yeah. I can tell you that half the women in this town got married simply to stop him asking them. It's the only possible defence. He does stop at that. He has standards. Limited ones, but still. You could pretend to be married, buy a cheap ring..."

Penny laughed. "What a horrible man. They said that David Hart was a ladies' man…" she added, fishing hopefully for more information.

Cath was not to be drawn into it. "Not like Warren is. Warren is ever hopeful, whereas somehow David Hart did manage to keep a lady friend from time to time. He was never a womaniser. Ignore the gossip. Anyway, I will see you tomorrow night, at my place, seven o'clock."

"Do I have to bring anything? Wine, snacks?"

"Not at all! Just yourself, that's all." Cath smiled warmly. "I must get on. The kids will be killing each other by now, and hubby will be barricading himself into the shed. It is a good job we don't have close neighbours."

Penny waved goodbye, feeling curiously warm and at the same time, bereft. Cath was lovely but her world was a different one to what Penny was used to.

Just like her sister, Ariadne, Penny thought. Family life, kids, all that. Except the Ariadne doesn't seem half as happy with it as Cath does.

I ought to tell Ariadne that I've moved, I suppose.

* * * *

Penny walked home with an aimless, slow step. She was lost in thought. There was a part of herself that was amazed and appalled that she was considering going to a kitchenware party, but she recognised her own snobbery in that. What was wrong with wanting to meet other people? She had not expected to be attending the opera and discussing Nietzsche every night, had she? She knew she needed to get over herself.

And remember, she told herself sternly. This was all about de-stressing, relaxing, letting go and becoming one with … one with … one with myself. As it were. Reconnecting with my creative and idealist side. I am going there with an open mind and I will meet some lovely people.

But when she reached her own cottage, the figure on the step, listening to Kali bark her own head off from within, made Penny's stomach clench.

What on earth was that Francine Black doing here?

CHAPTER FIVE

Francine greeted Penny with a frantic wave, as if somehow Penny could miss the apparition in layers of floral fabrics. She had a small bag at her feet, and an enormous hat on her head. Her smile was wide and warm. You couldn't look at a smile like that and not respond. She had one of those faces that shouldn't have worked; technically, she was a plain woman, with a long nose that was bulbous at the end, and uneven teeth, and narrow eyes. But her beaming grin made everyone feel so warm that if you had the choice, at a party, to talk to her or a supermodel, you'd always pick Francine. Penny smiled in spite of her surprise.

"You-hoo!" Francine warbled.

"Goodness. Hi, Francine. How did you…"

"I asked Daisy who asked Ash who said that Billy Choudhury knew but he didn't but his wife did. So here I am! I couldn't resist. What a beautiful cottage! Is your dog all right?"

Kali was apparently trying to eat her way through the wooden door in her excitement at having visitors. "Stand back, please," Penny said to Francine.

As soon as the door swung open, Kali burst through and launched herself in delight at Francine, who screamed and fell backwards, holding her arms over her face. "Get it off, get it off…"

Kali stood over the cowering woman, her tail and indeed her hips waggling in greeting, nuzzling Francine's face and hands.

"Oh, Kali, come here."

Kali licked Francine's wrist and reluctantly came to Penny's side. She tried not to laugh as Francine sat up, but when she saw Francine's face, her humour died.

"Are you all right? I didn't think you were scared of dogs. I'm so sorry. She really has no manners."

"It's a Rottweiler! It's a dangerous dog!" Francine said, her face pale and her hands trembling. Penny felt sick with shame, and also with anger at being unfairly labelled.

"She's not dangerous at all. I did say stand back …

she's just over excited. I'm really sorry. Are you all right? Are you hurt?"

Francine stayed on the ground, looking at Kali. Kali looked back, her head cocked to one side, her tail thumping on the ground.

"I'm not hurt," Francine said at last. "Gosh. I was so shocked. Wow. What a dog … she is pretty, though. I've never been this close to one before. Hello, beautiful."

"Yes, she is. Come on. I think you need a cup of tea."

Francine struggled to her feet, her bouncy nature temporarily subdued as she followed Penny into the cottage.

* * * *

Two bottles of wine later, and Penny couldn't remember why she'd disliked Francine, and Francine couldn't remember why she'd disliked the dog. They all sprawled across the living room floor as the height of the sofa had grown increasingly risky as more alcohol was consumed. Instead they lay on a plethora of cushions, giggling at childish jokes. Kali didn't giggle, exactly, but she seemed to get immense pleasure from making the two humans laugh. She'd roll over and over, waving her paws in the air until she got a reaction.

"London isn't the same without you," Francine said.

"You're repeating yourself. You said that before."

"Yeah but I'm drunk so I can."

"We're both drunk. Oh, aren't we too old to get drunk?"

"Too old! Nonsense. Sense. None. No sense." Francine snickered. "You're only as old as the man you feel. Felt any nice men?"

"Only a dead one," Penny said, her mood shifting from hysterical to maudlin with the alacrity that only a tipsy woman could manage. "Oh dear. Oh dear oh dear."

Francine reached out and patted Penny's thigh. Kali rolled over and her tongue lolled out of her mouth. Penny had to smile.

Francine said, as seriously as her slurred speech could manage, "It must have been awful. How did he die?"

"Electrocuted."

"No. Never!"

"But not by his electric fence."

"Murdered!" That thought sobered Francine up quickly. "There's a murderer here?" She looked around as if someone was about to burst through the door wearing a balaclava.

"Yes, there possibly is. Unless it was a strange suicide. Or an accident."

"Oh ... so, what are you going to do about it?"

"Lock my doors at night, and stay off private land. More wine?"

"I could really murder a cheese toastie. Oh, Penny, can I stay over tonight please?"

"I kind of assumed that you were."

Francine grinned sappily. "Thank you!"

* * * *

It was an evening of conversations started and aborted, circular arguments and random observations. But the next morning, as they both hunched over the kitchen table with narrowed eyes and tried to eat some dry toast and painkillers, the question of the murder resurfaced.

Francine had come prepared to stay overnight, and was wearing a fluffy pink bathrobe that made her hung-over pallid skin look even more deathly pale. She clutched a cup of hot coffee and whimpered. "Penny, aren't you worried that there's a killer on the loose?"

"Not really. I think, if he was murdered, it was a targeted attack. It must have been someone he knew, who had a reason for it. I don't believe that anyone else has to worry."

"I'd worry." Francine's eyes were slits against the light but she blinked rapidly in excitement. "What are you going to do?"

"Ah, yes, well, I do have a plan." In spite of her thumping head, furry mouth and queasy stomach, Penny was feeling upbeat and chipper. She was actually enjoying spending time with Francine. She'd been awful to work with – her relentless enthusiasm had been tiring – but socially? She was a delight. Now Penny was away from London, she was starting to see what an unpleasant person she had been becoming. Thank goodness she escaped when she did. She said, "It gives me something to follow. I'm going to buy the local newspaper and study it and find out about the area, and make an effort to talk with people and learn who is who."

Francine furrowed her brow. "No, that's not what I

meant at all. How are you going to find the murderer?"

Penny snorted a laugh most inelegantly. "How can I find a murderer? I could go and knock on doors, I suppose. 'Hi, I'm new here. Did you kill David Hart?' Yes, I am sure that would endear me to the locals."

"You found the body! You have a duty. You always stood up for what was right. That's why I liked working with you."

"I think I mostly stood up for my own interests. Francine, how are you still so lovely? London life was making me nasty."

Francine shrugged. "Oh, people are people. Everyone loves someone, don't they? I just look for that love in them. Hey, do you remember when we were in Berlin?"

"I remember that rather startling club. Why?"

"You stood up to that man, then, who was bullying the poor make-up girl. You were fantastic."

Penny thought back. Yes, she did remember. He'd accused her of spilling his pint. She hadn't. It was obvious. But no one spoke out except Penny. "I did what I had to do."

"You see!" Francine declared in triumph. "And it's the

same with this murder. Anyway, you're up to your neck in events already."

Penny remembered, then, some of the reasons that she'd disliked working with Francine. Her enthusiasm was so smothering. She rolled her itchy eyes. "It is absolutely nothing to do with me, and I need to leave it to the professionals."

"Rubbish! Everyone knows that amateur detectives are far more effective."

"Such as?"

"Er … Miss Marple?"

"Francine, I've got some really bad news and I know this is hard to take, but Miss Marple isn't real. Oh, and there's something I need to tell you about Santa Claus…"

Francine waved her right hand in the air dismissively. She had always made reality fit what she wanted to see. "I know that, but even so, it's true."

"It is not."

"You've got to find out who did it!"

"I have not."

Francine sat back, and said, somewhat smugly, "Well – what else are you doing with your time?"

* * * *

Francine left in the mid-morning. She had warmly embraced Penny, as if they were long-lost friends, and Penny patted her in return. Francine even gave Kali a cuddle, and apologised to the dog for calling her dangerous. Kali sneezed.

"I think too much," Penny told Kali once they were alone. "It was lovely of her to come and see me. I really hated working with her but she means well. It's a person's intentions that are important, isn't it? I didn't see that side of her before. My perception was all skewed."

Kali cocked her head.

"No, you don't understand, do you?" she said sadly, feeling the house was suddenly empty. "Come on. Let me get dressed. I suppose I should take you for a walk…"

She didn't leave the house until midday and she felt reluctant to face the possibility of meeting other dogs. However, she had to take responsibility. "Why are you so reactive?" she grumbled to Kali as they made their way out of the cottage. "Why are you so aggressive?"

Suddenly Penny stopped dead, and Kali lurched against the lead. Perception. It was all about perception. "*Are* you aggressive?" she asked the dog.

Kali sniffed the ground.

"Maybe, maybe not." They continued on. "Maybe you're just scared."

* * * *

"Right. I can do this. Francine told me to, after all," Penny muttered to herself. Francine had, indeed, insisted that Penny attend the kitchenware party. It would be "a blast" and "a scream", apparently. She stood outside Cath's detached house, still feeling the lingering effects of the previous night's drinking clouding her tender head. The house stood in a remote spot halfway between Upper Glenfield and Lincoln, set back from the main road and hidden by tall cypress trees and conifers. Lincolnshire seemed littered with square, boxy houses, standing alone and isolated and surrounded by fields and dark, intimidating hedges, just like this.

There were half a dozen cars on the wide gravel

driveway, and all the windows were lit and welcoming.

She'd had agonies about what to wear and had changed her clothes four times until she'd had a severe word with herself and settled on black trousers and a patterned blouse. Her bony knees meant she would never wear short skirts, and long skirts made her feel alarmingly hippy-like. The black trousers reminded her of her confident, corporate days. Still she felt a little nervous as she pressed the bell. In London, she could flounce into a room and charm everyone. Here it seemed different. This was not her familiar territory.

Cath flung the door open and her wide smile instantly made everything all right. "Come in! Now then! I'm so glad you came. Please. This way. Oh, don't worry about taking your shoes off. I've got kids. For your own sake, you'll want to keep them on. Plasticine, ugh. Shoes are the least of my worries – here we are. Can I get you a drink?"

"I'm driving. A softie, please. Do you have any lemonade?" She was never, ever drinking again, anyway, she promised herself and her liver. Never.

She found herself in a long lounge, with a table at one end that bristled with bottles and plates of nibbles. There were two overstuffed three-seater sofas, two matching armchairs that seemed to have been inflated and then smothered with cushions, and a selection of chairs brought in from the kitchen, the dining room, and possibly from outside on the patio if the plastic ones were any clue.

She recognised the beehive-wearing woman from the gossip in the bakery aisle at the mini-market. There were four other women there, all clutching drinks and smiling with open, friendly faces, and plenty of unashamed curiosity. Cath did a brief introduction, missing out exactly how they'd met under awkward circumstances, and everyone chorused hello.

The beehive woman, who was revealed to be the local hairdresser and called Agatha, patted the spare seat next to her on the three-seater. "Now then, come here, my love. I have seen you before, haven't I? Eh?"

"Yes. I think I interrupted your conversation. In the mini-market?"

"That's right! I remember. I saw you again but you were talking to Warren. Or at least, he was talking to you."

Penny bit her lip. In a small town like this, she didn't want to speak badly of a man who might turn out to be someone's uncle or brother or secret crush. "Yes. He's quite a ... *determined* sort of man."

Agatha howled with laughter, and announced to the whole group, "You hear that? You hear what she said, eh? Warren's a determined sort of man!" She turned back to Penny and patted her on the knee as if Penny were five years old. "Now you listen to me, my love. He's a horrible pest of a man who doesn't understand 'no' and I am sure he means no harm but don't you encourage him, you hear."

"I wasn't encouraging him at all!"

Someone else said, "Yeah, Agatha, that's not fair. A woman only has to be breathing to encourage Warren."

"I did tell him no. Anyway, it's not all bad. Warren is the reason I'm here, to be honest," Penny confessed. Cath was standing close by and she grinned.

"Yes, he was coming after both of us, wasn't he?" she said. "We evaded him pretty well."

"Yes. I was avoiding him which is why I kept on asking you about this party," Penny said.

"You wouldn't have come if Warren hadn't been pursuing you?" Cath raised an eyebrow in mock indignation.

"Well ... it's not something I've ever done before."

"There's always a first time!" Agatha gurgled, making it sound like a filthy joke, and everyone laughed.

Cath began to set out some interesting and innovative new plastic kitchen products while the rest of the women continued to drink and chat. Some of the items looked frighteningly similar to the things Penny had seen at the more "adult" party she'd unwillingly attended. She didn't like to ask what the long thin yellow thing, with the spiral on the end, was designed to do.

Instead, Penny said to Agatha, "Speaking of unpleasant men, and I don't like to speak ill of the dead, but can you tell me more about David Hart, that farmer who was … found dead? Was he ever married at all?"

"No, he never married, but he had his share of lovers!" Agatha said. "Isn't that right? What about that latest floozy on his arm—"

"Now, Agatha, that's not fair. I liked Mary," someone said.

"Mary!" Agatha snorted. "Her. Huh. No better than she should be, that one!"

It was a curious phrase that Penny thought she understood without really making sense of it. "Did he really have a lot of … lovers?"

"I don't know," Cath said. "I actually think it's a lot of gossip with not a lot of truth. He had a few girlfriends from time to time, but honestly, he wasn't parading up and down the High Street with them. He kept himself to himself, mostly. Everything else is mere speculation." She spoke firmly and warningly.

Agatha sucked at her teeth. "Maybe. But he *was* seeing Mary, most recently. That's true, isn't it? That Mary Radcliffe from along North Road. All jingly bracelets. She thinks she's something but she's not. Eh!"

Someone with a little more heart and feeling said, "I wonder how she's taking it? His death, I mean. They might not have been married but even so. It must be hard."

There was a moment of respectful silence, and even Agatha looked abashed. "True, true. A difficult situation for anyone, under the circumstances. I wonder how he died …" Agatha petered out but looked quizzically at Cath, who shook her head.

"No. No idea. I'm not at work right now. Read the paper tomorrow. Let's look at these pots! Have you ever seen an egg timer like *this?*"

No, Penny had not. She had thought it was a lemon squeezer. Penny was glad that the conversation was being steered away from the topic of the murder. Fascinated as she was by the rumours and gossip, the fact was that a man was dead – and she had touched him. She shuddered. It didn't matter that he was single, or a womaniser, or any such thing. Some people's lives would now be missing a piece. A family was bereaved.

However, though she no longer wanted to talk about David Hart, the figure of Mary, his last girlfriend, did intrigue her. "Does Mary work?" she asked, thinking it was likely to be a safe topic of conversation.

Cath's face looked up, startled, as Agatha laughed again, and said, "Oh, she's here and there! Eh? She's doing those cards now, isn't she? She's always been into that craft stuff. Jewellery and cards and what have you. Glue a feather onto a bit of paper and write 'peace' in swirly pen, and charge three quid, eh. My kids did better at primary school."

"I bought a sundial off her," someone said. "It was made from a bit of slate. It wasn't bad till the sticky-out bit fell off."

"Well, she certainly needs the cash," Agatha said.

"Ooh! Is that one of those things that does nuts?"

Cath passed her the fluorescent yellow plastic thing that looked more like a small rocket. Quite what it was supposed to do to nuts was anyone's guess. Penny sat back and pondered what she had learned. Would Mary be named in the will? It depended on how recent a girlfriend she was. Was she more? A partner, a lover. If she needed cash, she could have…

No. She pushed it out of her mind. It wasn't her business.

Agatha was waving the nut-mangling thing at her. "Have you ever seen the like? See how it moves!"

"Er…"

Someone else was cooing about a knife sharpener, and the chance to talk more about Mary was lost.

* * * *

The kitchenware party lasted a lot longer than Penny had expected. She had ended up buying some multi-coloured stackable storage boxes and a cleaning cloth with micro-something embedded in it, that promised miracles just short of getting up and doing the dusting itself. Even though she hadn't had any alcoholic drink, she felt warm and fuzzy as she said goodbye to the gathering of women and got into her car. It had been two good nights for her in a row. She felt mellow.

Cath was the last to say goodbye. The police detective had become progressively more relaxed and then raucous as the night had progressed, and increasingly incautious about what she said. She had regaled them with some lurid tales about how criminals smuggled mobile phones which made everyone cross their legs as their eyes watered.

Cath leaned through the open car window as Penny started the engine and got the heaters going. "Thank you so much for coming," she said. There was the tinge of alcohol on her breath.

"Thanks for the invite. I mean it, in spite of my reservations. I really enjoyed myself. Cath, can I ask … has it been established yet whether David Hart's death, that electrocution, was accidental? Or a suicide? Or a … murder?"

Cath shook her head and smiled. "I'm not allowed to say. But no, it wasn't. It was foul play." She clamped a hand over her mouth. "I didn't say that, right! You'll get me into trouble. Go home!"

"I'm sorry. Thank you. Get inside before you get cold."

Penny's mind was a whirl as she drove home. David Hart *had* been murdered. It was true.

Somewhere in Upper Glenfield, a murderer was on the loose. And she had found the body! That made her involved. Francine's words came back to her. She *was* up to her neck in events.

It sort of made her a suspect, she thought, as she pulled up outside her cottage. I'm a newcomer to the town too.

She felt a tingle of butterflies in her stomach. She got out of the car and smiled to herself. I've made friends and now I have a purpose. I *will* find the murderer. Things have to be put right. This is great. Things are going to work out just fine.

She remained happy until she opened the front door and saw the devastation that Kali had wreaked through her home.

CHAPTER SIX

Thursday opened with torrential rain hammering on the roof and bursting from a hole in the guttering, and Penny was delighted. No one walked their dogs in the rain; she and Kali would have a free run of the town. She layered up with new yellow waterproofs and sallied forth. She would have danced and sung a song like a terrible old musical if she knew all the words to anything. Kali seemed surprised at Penny's exuberance, and behaved impeccably after about twenty minutes of insistent pulling. Penny was discovering that in the battle of wills, she may as well accept that Kali was stronger; so instead of letting the dog dictate where they were going, Penny would stop, and turn around, every time Kali pulled forwards. Eventually Kali realised that pulling got her nowhere. She still tried to pull, but with less heart, and the walk back home was actually fun. Kali was still a pest, but Penny was beginning to feel possessive of her. Kali was *her* pest.

Penny spent another hour attempting to sort out the broadband to her cottage. She rang around all the suppliers, found she was restricted in who would service the cottage, and had to concede an expensive defeat. Then she decided she needed to unearth more old, shabby dog-walking clothes. She was developing a line on the thigh of her jeans that was where Kali's slobbery jowls pressed against her when she wanted treats and fussing. She went to root about in some of the unpacked boxes in the spare room. To her surprise, she unearthed a decades-old sketchbook in the bottom of a box of winter clothes. It reminded her of her student days once more, and she felt warm. It inspired her to get sketching again. She brought the book down to the kitchen and was just leafing through it when there was a knock at her front door.

She wondered if it might be Francine, back with more advice and wine. She held firmly onto Kali's collar with one hand as she opened the door slightly with the other, shouting through, "It's okay, she's friendly... probably ... are you wearing a hat?"

"Er, no, should I be? I can put my coat over my head."
It was Drew's voice, and Penny perked up with relief.

"Hello there! How did you know where I lived?" she
asked as she opened the door fully and Kali was released
to greet him. Her whole body seemed to wag as she dashed
up to the man.

"Everyone knows where the new London woman
lives. We know all your business, remember? Your friend
has gone home, then?"

"That is just creepy. And yes, she has, thank goodness.
My liver is hanging by a thread now. How is it that everyone
knows who I've got visiting me, but no one knows about
David Hart?" she asked suspiciously.

"You're new and exciting. You're being watched."

Eww. "I don't know if I like the sound of that." Let's
watch to see what the mad London woman with the
dangerous dog does next, she thought. That's not fair.

"You do like it, or you wouldn't have moved here. It's
what people come to small towns for. Your business is
everyone's business, now. This is called neighbourhood
spirit."

She was suddenly aware that he was standing in the

rain and she jumped back into the hallway. "Please, come in."

He stepped into the porch, shaking the drops from his hair, and pulled a bag out of his large raincoat pocket. "I won't come in and drip everywhere. I just wanted to give you this. I think you might find it useful, with the dog."

She took it and unwrapped the bag to find a collection of straps and a metal circle. "What is it?" she asked, shaking it out. Flashbacks to the adult party came to mind.

"It's a head-collar for Kali. I reckon it's the right size. She's only got a narrow head, hasn't she, for a Rottie? I mean, it might not work, or you might want to try a different way, or a harness, or whatever, but it's worth a try."

"Oh! How lovely. I don't know about the fit … look, come on through. You can't stand in the porch. Come to the kitchen. I'll put the kettle on. And, thank you. So kind."

He kicked off his wellington boots, leaving them in the puddle they had already formed, and followed her to the back of the house, Kali getting underfoot as they went.

"Settling in?" he asked.

"Yes, thanks." She realised with some shame that the

two empty wine bottles from two nights previously were still standing by the back door, waiting to be taken out to the recycling area. He was going to think her some kind of alcoholic, so she pre-empted that by nodding at them and saying, "Ahh … my friend, she, er … she brought them as a gift …"

He smiled. "A cheeky red there. She has good taste. What did she think to Glenfield, then?"

"I don't know. We didn't actually leave the living room. I was amazed she came, to be honest. She kind of tracked me down against my will."

"What?" Drew took his coat off and folded it so the wet outer layer was on the inside.

"I didn't tell her where I lived. She was one of those people who seemed to hang on to me and I couldn't shake her off. We worked together but she was … annoying. Wow. I sound like a silly school girl, don't I?"

"Yes," he said, and she blushed with shame.

"I am petty," she said.

"Yes," he agreed.

"Er … no, you're supposed to say nice things that are lies, just to make me feel better." Especially as you don't even know me, she thought.

"Nope. I'm not going to do that." He shrugged. "But I did bring you a head-collar, so there's that."

"Thank you," she said. She had to laugh. "So how does this head-collar thing work, then?"

He knelt down and encouraged Kali to sniff it. "I noticed how you struggled to hold her back the other day, and it made me think about my work with horses. They put a collar on if a horse needs to pull a cart or plough, right? So the animal can use all their strength. And Rotties, they were used to pull carts, back in Germany. All their strength comes from their chest. But the head-collar means she can't put her full weight into pulling you over. Just take care with it. Don't use one of them retracting leads or you'll hurt her neck. And don't yank at her. Mind you, you shouldn't be yanking at her with a normal collar on."

"Collars are designed for dogs, though, aren't they?"

"It's my understanding that dogs have something called the oppositional reflex," he said, the long words clumsy in his mouth. "I mean, you pull and they pull back. It's automatic. So dragging on the lead won't get you anywhere." He patted Kali's shoulder. "What do you think, there? Smells okay, doesn't it?"

Kali tentatively put her nose into the smaller loop. Drew rubbed her ears and gave her some more praise. "Do you have any treats that she likes?"

"No, I don't want her to get fat."

Drew sighed and remained crouching, but he looked up at her with a serious expression. "You don't really know me and all that, but I kind of feel I need to speak my mind about the dog thing. Er…"

"Please do. I mean, you haven't held back so far … Tell me. I need help, I know…" Oh, be gentle, she added in her head. I want to get it right but don't tell me I'm wrong too harshly. "Okay, you don't have to lie to make me feel good."

"Okay. I won't. It's about the dog, not you. So, it's like this. How will she know if she's done something right?"

"I say good girl."

"Does she like food? And treats?"

"My goodness, yes. She won't stop eating."

"If two people wanted you to do two different things, and when you did one thing, person A said 'well done' and when you did the other thing, person B gave you a cake, who will you want to please?"

"Person B. Cake, always." Penny could already see where Drew was going.

"If Kali is motivated by food, use that motivation. She won't get fat if you adjust her main meals. If she puts the head-collar on, give her a treat and take it off again. Bit by bit she'll learn that the head-collar means good things."

"But if I give her treats for everything, I'll be feeding her all the time!"

"At first, yes, you will. Use her meal as treats. Why not? Then reduce it. Anyway, she'll soon learn that the head-collar means walks. Please, do try it. Otherwise you'll be telling her off more than you reward her, and how can that make her happy?"

It wouldn't make anyone happy, she thought. It made sense. "Okay, I'll try it, I promise. Thank you so much."

"Great." He got to his feet and grinned. "Rewards always work better than punishment."

"How's work? Where do you have you ... uh, what's it called? Smithy? You said you were a blacksmith, sort of."

"Yeah, I have a smithy. Actually it's an industrial unit at the end of the High Street."

"How marvellous! I'd love to look round one day. If that would be okay."

"You think it's going to look like a romantic Victorian painting, don't you?" He laughed. "You can certainly come round. Work is quiet though. I don't shoe many horses, and I tend to travel to do that on-site. Horses aren't my thing, to be honest. Their teeth are enormous. No, I mostly end up doing ornamental ironwork. And I'm competing against imports, and it's a tough business."

She looked again at him. The jeans were no-brand and faded, his socks had holes, and his sweater was baggy in the wrong places. "I'm sorry to hear that. How do you mean, that you're a 'sort of' blacksmith?"

"Ahh, well, I realised I needed to diversify, you see. If smithing isn't paying – and it's not – I decided to make a change. I've been developing some field-craft sessions with the local hotel, The Arches. It's kind of a conference centre too, and they already do things like hawking and off-road driving."

"That sounds amazing! So you're like a tracker or something?"

"Yes, pretty much. Oh – now, that's beautiful. It can't

be local…"

His eye had caught the stack of sketches that she'd left on the kitchen table.

"No, that's somewhere in Kent."

"Did you draw these?" He got closer but was too polite to reach out and touch them.

"I did. But it was years ago." She felt embarrassed and exposed. Showing someone a picture she had deemed fit for public view was one thing – having her half-formed sketches spied upon was like being caught in your worst nearly-wash-day underwear. She wanted to scoop them up and hide them.

He smiled. "You have a talent. I love being out in the countryside, walking, but I can't even take a decent photo of what I see. Hey. Would you like to try Kali with the head-collar?"

"It's raining."

"It's easing off, and you'll not dissolve, I'm sure. Are you made of sugar? We don't have to go far. I'll show you how to persuade her it's a good thing. Have you any ham you could chop up for treats?"

Less than ten minutes later, they were walking slowly

through the light rain but not going the usual way towards the centre of town. Instead, Drew turned left out of her cottage and took them towards the end of the row, which Penny thought was a dead end. She'd never even walked that way, because she would have felt daft getting to the end, and turning around.

"There's a path here," he told her. "It cuts down to the river and under the bridge where the kids hang out in summer. And then out into hillier land, westwards."

It didn't matter that the rain was soaking everything. The sky wasn't dark; patches of blue shone brightly through grey clouds. As well as the grey slabs, there were occasional white fluffy bundles, moving quite quickly up above their heads. The fields were already carpeted with green and yellow. She could almost imagine the rain being sucked up into the stems of the crops, growing and blooming visibly before her eyes.

By the river, the land was muddy but Drew seemed to avoid ever sinking into the bogs, whereas Penny was constantly up to her ankles. "Are you some kind of earth wizard?" she complained.

He looked back and laughed when he saw her, stuck

as she was in an unexpected pool of water. "Don't step in the boggy bits," he said.

"It's *all* boggy bits," she replied crossly. "Apart from the bits you magically know to step on."

He pointed at the dark green spears of foliage. "See those rushes? They like water. It's a clue. That clump of yellower grass there, that will be fine to walk on. Take a leap onto it."

She jumped to the patch of grass and found her feet land on soft but solid ground. They continued on, Penny watching carefully, and learning where to walk. She felt like some kind of old-world tracker. She wanted to go on one of his field-craft courses now.

"Speaking of clues," she said to Drew's back. "What do you think to the death of David Hart?"

"A tragic accident, for sure. And a horrible way to go. They say he was electrocuted by his fence!"

"It wasn't an accident and it probably wasn't his fence. I happen to know that he was murdered."

"No. Really?" Drew stopped dead and turned. "How do you know?"

"I was told by … a police officer," she said cautiously.

"Oh, that Cath blabbed, did she? Get a drink inside her and she's anybody's. So to speak. Well, well. So, who did it?"

"That's the thing," Penny said. "They don't know! Perhaps a serial killer is on the loose!"

"Not here in Upper Glenfield. Anyway, most murders are accidental, aren't they? Like, manslaughter stuff. The situation is usually that one bloke pushes another bloke in a pub, he falls down and hits his head, and boom – dead. The bloke that pushed him is then liable for manslaughter."

"Maybe. Or *maybe* this was premeditated. You are a proper local. Who would want David Hart dead, do you think? You know all my business, apparently."

"Are you a part time police officer, now?"

"No," she said. "I want something to do and I did find the body, so I'm linked. I'm connected. And I thought perhaps an outsider like myself could bring a fresh eye..."

"You're having crime investigation fantasies, aren't you?"

She shook her head stubbornly, but had to agree. It was all Francine's fault for encouraging her. Now the idea was in her head, she couldn't shift it. "No. Yes. Maybe.

There was one time in Dusseldorf where someone was stealing from the canteen truck and I worked out who it was... maybe I have a gift for it."

He rolled his eyes. "You'll get into trouble."

She shrugged. "I know I'm being facetious but really, I'm just using it as a way to get to know people and the community. It's a great conversation opener. I was at a kitchenware party last night and they were all talking about it."

"A kitchenware party?" he said. "Is that a cover-up for something else? No, don't answer that, let me live in ignorance. Look, my advice is, don't listen to gossip and rumour. It's got more than one person into bother here in Glenfield. Someone lost their job over it not so long back."

"Did they? Oh dear." They continued walking, side by side. "But listen. You told me about the ramblers and that guy called Ed. He's a prime suspect, isn't he?"

"No one would kill over the question of access to a footpath! Would they?"

"Maybe, maybe not," she said. "I've seen footage on the news of protestors. People get really angry about local issues. I was involved in the documentary about the shade of pink someone painted their house in Cornwall. It got really rather heated. Some people did end up in court. And the other thing is, what about the dead man's brother? Thomas, isn't it? I had heard that they argued." Okay, she had to admit to herself. That *was* pure gossip overheard in the mini-market.

But Drew agreed. "They didn't get on at all but there always seems to be more to it than just sibling rivalry. There was some kind of silent bitterness. Oh, listen to me... I'm as bad as the rest of them."

"It's just community spirit and neighbourly interest; it's fine," she reassured him. "Who was the older brother of the two?"

"Thomas was."

"Were there any other siblings?"

"Nope, just David and Thomas."

She persisted with her questions. "Did David inherit the farm or did he buy it?"

Drew thought for a moment. "He inherited it, but I don't really know why it went to him and not Thomas, being as he was the older one. Except ... okay, thinking about it, maybe it was because Thomas was never very interested in any of that. He went off to join the Army and then he worked all over the world, as some kind of close protection officer."

"Wow, that sounds glamorous."

"Not so much, any more. He was Glenfield's golden boy once, apparently. He's a night security guard in Lincoln now, at some scrap yard."

"He could be a suspect."

"Maybe," Drew concurred. "And what about Mary, his partner? Girlfriend? What do you call that kind of relationship? Girlfriend sounds too ... immature, you know, for teenagers."

"And lover sounds a bit ... yeah, I don't know. Anyway, whatever. Girlfriend. She was a recent girlfriend, too, from what I hear. Why would she kill him? I don't think she had time to get to that stage of a relationship. You know, that point when you realise you want to kill the other person because they leave their toe nail clippings in a pile on the bedside table."

They stopped while Kali decided to mark her spot. Penny sighed and pulled out a plastic bag.

Drew looked up at the brightening sky, and mused to

himself, "It's always about love, money or power, isn't it, in the end?"

"That's a good point!" Penny said. "I need to make a chart of all this. I need coloured marker pens and a really big bit of paper."

"Are you sure? Look. Supposing there is a murderer. The thing about murderers is, uh ... well, they are murderers, right? They are outside the law. They're kind of dangerous. So…"

"I'm just following the case and thinking about stuff. I can do that," she protested.

"There's a look on your face that worries me," Drew said. "Like you're going to start digging around for stuff. I know you said you have the advantage, being an outsider, but that means you don't know who you can ask and who you can't. Don't forget that a lot of people have lived here for generations and some of their enmities go back generations, too. You could end up in proper bother."

"I'll be fine." Penny felt annoyed. She had hoped Drew would be an ally, helping her sift through the clues, but if he was just going to tell her not to ask questions, he was no help at all. "So, where does this path lead?"

"You're changing the subject."

"Yes, I am."

"Hmm."

They faced one another, and she stared at him. Yes, he had brought her a head-collar for Kali and yes, it was working fantastically well, and it occurred to her that she owed him some money for it. But ultimately she wasn't going to let herself be deterred from something she really wanted to do.

He crumbled first. "We'll carry on a little way past the bridge," he said at last. "I'll show you. It's a nice walk when it isn't raining."

"It's a nice walk anyway," she said. "And thank you so much for taking the time out to walk with me. I do really appreciate it. And the head-collar. And everything."

He was walking beside her but he flashed her a sideways smile. "You're welcome. I'm just doing my bit to show that our villages and towns aren't the stereotype of unfriendly locals."

As long as they don't ask questions, she thought to herself. But she smiled back.

CHAPTER SEVEN

Penny woke up on Friday morning feeling determined to get to the bottom of the murder case.

Thank you, Francine, she thought. You are right. I've misjudged you ... Penny still didn't want to work with her, and was glad she wouldn't have Francine as a colleague again, but she'd opened Penny's eyes. She made a mental note to send her a surprise gift of expensive champagne in a hamper. Then she felt warm and fuzzy. And that was certainly nicer than feeling stressed and confused.

Yes. Today will be a good day, she decided, humming in the shower and almost dancing around her bedroom.

Kali was surprised and a little peeved that she got less food that morning, and stayed stuck to Penny's side as she chopped up some sandwich ham and put it in a paper envelope in her coat pocket. The dog's big eyes followed every movement of the knife.

"Yes, it is for you, but only when you're good," Penny told the drooling dog.

She took some deep, calming breaths as she clipped the head-collar onto Kali. After the horrible incidents where Kali had launched herself at passing dogs, Penny had found that she dwelled on them more and more, building them up in her mind until she felt quite sick at the thought of going out.

Now, she knew that when she tensed up at the sight of another dog, she was transmitting her own anxiety to Kali, and Kali was sent into protective mode – on top of her own fear. She didn't need a trainer to work with Kali, Penny thought. She needed someone to train herself first.

She patted Kali and rested her head against her shoulders for a second. "It will be okay," she said to both herself and the dog.

Then she stood up and took another calming breath. "Right. Come on, you. Let's go."

As she walked, she tried to swing with a confident stride. Drew had outlined his theory on the way back the previous day; it was him who had suggested that Kali's reaction might be rooted in fear. "You need to make her feel that seeing other dogs is a really good thing," he had said. "Like people take them to the vets for no reason, just for treats, so they associate it with good things. Eventually, in her head, seeing a dog will trigger her to look at you for a yummy treat."

It was a theory that she liked. She resolved to put it into practise.

The small town was all fresh and sparkling after the days of rain. The sun was shining and it finally felt like a promising spring day. There were tubs lining the open market area, and tulips waved their showy heads in a riot of colour. She discovered that market day was Friday, and the central area was busy with shoppers and stalls selling watch batteries, mop buckets, huge packets of chocolate, strange 1950's aprons in polyester gingham, and a fish seller who had a PA system rigged up at the back of his refrigerated lorry.

She was still nervous about walking Kali with so much distraction there, and she avoided going directly past the market. They turned right and headed out of town, along their now-usual route to the Spinney and beyond. At one point they saw another dog in the distance, and Kali tensed, her ears flattening and her hackles rising. Instantly, Penny grabbed a handful of ham and began offering it to Kali in a cheerful voice, her hand shaking and spilling the tasty meat all over the pavement.

Kali was on it immediately, the other dog forgotten as she searched for every last scrap of meat.

"Oh. Oh! Good girl. Good girl," Penny said, in wonderment. So, some things were more important to Kali than other dogs – food was a great motivator.

She walked along deep in thought.

Everyone has their motivation. Drew said it was love, money or power.

David Hart had love – Mary, at least. Money? Perhaps. They said the farm was doing well. What about power?

I need to do some research, she thought.

* * * *

She got back to her cottage and Kali flopped, exhausted, on the living room rug, and sighed as her eyes closed. Penny had worked hard to get Kali to walk nicely on the lead, and it was clear that the unexpected mental exertion was as tiring as the physical exercise.

She decided she needed to work on following the clues that she had. She lined the suspects up in her head: Mary, the lover; Thomas, the brother; and Ed, the disgruntled rambler. Thomas interested her the most – she felt she knew least about him – and she decided to go and talk to Agatha.

After all, as the local hairdresser, she was bound to know all sorts of things. And though much of it might be classed as gossip, there could be grains of truth in it.

She left Kali with a rawhide bone to gnaw on, and went out to the salon, intending to make an appointment for some time later in the week. Then she planned to come home and make a list of questions and enquiries to ask Agatha at her appointment.

'Curl Up And Dye' was a small salon nestling between the butcher's shop and the mini-market. Penny scurried past the big windows of the mini-market, not wanting to attract Warren's unwelcome attention. There were huge black and silver posters in the windows of the salon, featuring glossy-haired models with digitally smoothed curls and faces like porcelain. She suspected the general clientele of the salon were after much more practical hair styles, on the whole.

The bell over the door jingled merrily as she entered. The three chairs down the left hand side were empty, and Agatha was at the back of the salon, sweeping up. She was dressed in black, head to toe, except for her gold lame mules and metallic silver nails.

"Now then, Londoner!" she sang out. "Penny, how are you, eh?"

"Hi, Agatha. I'm very well. How are you?" She wasn't wildly keen on being called "Londoner" but it was clear that Agatha meant no harm.

"My sciatica is playing me up rotten, and my salon washing machine went pop and bang this morning, and my husband used up all the milk on his cornflakes. Mustn't grumble, eh?"

"Er … right. No. Quite. Sorry about the … everything. I was wondering if I might book an appointment for a trim? And maybe a bit of a restyle? Something … funky."

"Any time, my love. Are you in a hurry right now?"

"No, no plans. I–"

But it wasn't a conversational politeness. Agatha meant something different. "Well, then, I can do you here and now! Would that suit you, my love? My next appointment isn't until three, and that's Mrs Hargreaves, and she'll be late. But she'll bring biscuits, so I don't mind that at all, eh."

Agatha put the sweeping brush aside and descended on Penny like a boulder rolling down a hill, with a slow inevitability, grabbing a gown as she came. Penny had wanted to prepare but now she was trapped.

No, she told herself sternly. I am not trapped. Here is an opportunity… Just think on your feet.

"Great!" she said brightly. "Wonderful. Thank you very much."

She could do this. After all, in her television career, she'd had to be so flexible they'd called her the rubber-band woman. If she could cope with trying to hire forty blue taxis in Mumbai with only three hours to do it in, she could deal with a sudden haircut.

And it was not only a chance to talk. This was another blow struck for her new, refreshed, relaxed self. No more sensible, professional hair styles! Maybe she'd have her hair coloured. Green? Red? Maybe platinum blonde, giving her dull usual strawberry blonde a startling shine?

Agatha patted a chair. "Can I get you a brew?"

Her instinct was to say no, because few people could make a decent cup of tea that she liked. She forced herself to accept. It would help the bonding, and make her look less of a stuck-up southerner, she told herself. "Yes, thank you, that would be lovely. Tea, with milk."

Agatha clipped the gown around her shoulders and pottered off, leaving Penny to stare at herself in the mirror. Usually the lights in a salon seemed expressly designed to make the clients look half-dead, with their harsh overhead glare and unflattering angles. Penny suddenly realised the salon was actually unlit. The sunlight streaming in through the window was the only illumination.

Then she heard voices from the back room, and with a click, Penny was flooded with light and the reflection of her features flattened and aged instantly. Great, she thought. I was enjoying pretending that I was ten years younger.

She avoided eye contact with herself while she waited for Agatha to re-emerge with the cup of tea. "Sorry about that, my love," she said as she popped it onto a small table near Penny's hand. "Like I say, the washing machine gave

116

up the ghost this morning. Bang! I nearly did a wee. I've got Ed in to look at it. Turns out to be a fuse in the plug socket so we had to have the power turned off."

"Ed …"

"Here he is!"

A skinny man with razor blade cheekbones and flat, dull blue eyes came into the salon, carrying a toolbox. He was wearing boots with no laces, and threadbare jeans that were artfully ripped horizontally all the way down both thighs in a style that Penny hadn't seen since the poodle haired glam rockers of the eighties.

"How do," he said, nodding politely at Penny. "Now then. All done, Agatha."

"Wonderful, thank you."

He nodded again to Penny, his eyes sliding over his face without even registering her, and then he was gone.

As soon as they had the salon to themselves, Penny wanted to leap in with her questions, but first she had to explain to Agatha she needed a vibrant, exciting, youthful style. Agatha smiled and nodded and said she knew exactly what Penny wanted. She seemed very confident, but Penny couldn't stifle her nervousness as Agatha set about combing through Penny's hair.

"So, who was that?" Penny asked, trying to keep her head still. "I have heard of someone called Ed who's into the ramblers. Is that him?"

"Oh, the very same. Edwin Montgomery. He leads a lot of local walks. Yes, he's pretty handy to have around the place."

"He looked a bit of a hippy, with that tie-dyed top. I haven't seen many of those around recently." Penny was moving her mental list of suspects around. So Ed could fix things, could he? That was a clue.

"Oh, yeah, for sure. He's not been in Glenfield that long but he was making his mark straight away. He's a yellowbelly anyway, you know, a proper native Lincolnshire lad. He organised a litter-picking group and they planted trees by the slipe and he writes to the paper all the time about windfarms. I can't remember if he's for them or against them, though. But he's awfully passionate, one way or the other. I wish I could have half his energy, eh!"

"Wow. So what's his job? Does he have an actual job?"

"Handyman, I suppose," Agatha said. "He does electrical stuff and basic plumbing and bits and pieces. Not gas. He can't do gas, apparently."

"That's interesting. And so he was fighting to get paths re-opened…?"

"Oh, he is always into something. Now, my love, how long do you want your fringe? I think we can sweep it up here and …"

"That's fine. Just out of my eyes, thanks."

Penny took a moment to rearrange her thoughts while she sipped her cooling tea, and Agatha tutted because she'd moved her head when she should have been still. Ed had a motive and he had the means to tamper with the fence.

Although she still wasn't sure if an electrical fence could be set to stun or kill. Cath had thought not. She'd insisted the fence wasn't to blame. But surely power was power? Whether it came from the mains or a battery pack, it was still electricity. She remembered something vague from school about alternating current and direct current, but the details were hazy.

Then she remembered she was here to find out about Thomas, David's brother, not try to recall high school physics. Drew had warned her not to ask questions. But how dangerous could it be? She put the cup of tea back on the table. "Agatha, what do you know about Thomas Hart, David's brother?"

It was the wrong kind of question, she realised instantly. It was too open and unfocused. "What do you want to know, my love?" Agatha said, tugging at a strand of hair for no apparent reason.

"I don't know." Well, did he kill his brother? Huh. Too direct. "They didn't get on, did they, David and Thomas?"

"Nope. They had nothing to do with one another. It's sad, eh? Families should stick together. Except for my husband's sister. She can stay away, thank you."

"Was it mutual dislike?" she asked. "Between Thomas and David, I mean. Not you and your sister-in-law."

"I reckon so, yeah. Thomas was older but I don't know what went on with them all at home because he upped sticks and went off to the Army as soon as he could. Tells you something, eh? He left that after a few years and travelled the world being some kind of bodyguard. All the girls fancied him whenever he came back to visit the family farm. He was all muscles and tan, and goodness, didn't he know it, but you don't mind them parading around when they're worth looking at, eh."

"Is that the family farm that David ran?"

"That's right. Their father died first, rest his soul, though he was a mean old codger, then their mother, lovely woman and a saint if you know what I mean, and David took it on. Thomas was never interested in it."

"And Thomas still lives in Upper Glenfield...?"

"Oh yes. Him and his snooty wife Eleanor live in a shiny detached house up on that estate, 'The Shires', all those boxy ticky-tacky houses for commuters and them as don't want to really *live* here. He works up in Lincoln now. He's some kind of night watchman at a scrap yard on the east side. Sorry, 'metal recycling plant'. Got to be politically correct, haven't I?"

Penny decided not to tackle Agatha about what "politically correct" really meant. "And what does Eleanor do?"

"Ha!" Agatha's scissors flashed with increasing venom around Penny's face and she regretted asking a potentially emotional question when she was so close to the sharp blades. "Ha. That one? She's done a little of this and a bit of that. But she never thought she'd need to work, you know. Everything was always above her. She came in here once because her regular woman in Lincoln was off on holiday but the face on her was like I'd rubbed pee in her hair."

"Gosh. Do they have children?"

"Oh yes, and they've escaped, and good luck to them. One's in Australia, which tells you everything you need to know about Eleanor, eh. The other is in Scotland. Clearly he'd rather freeze on a mountain than deal with his mother. Ha! So would I. That long enough at the back for you?"

"Yes, great, thanks." The style was choppy and slightly like a pixie, and to Penny's surprise, it seemed to work. She fell silent as she repeated all the information back to herself. Agatha patted her hair and sprayed her with something that smelled quite nice but didn't seem to make any discernible difference.

"Is the length okay for you at the sides now?"

"Yes, it's fantastic, really, thank you." She really was delighted, although she would have struggled to tell Agatha if it wasn't quite right. In London, she had had no qualms about letting a hairdresser know if they hadn't hit the right mark. But here, in the small town, it seemed far more awkward to speak up. "Honestly. Just what I wanted."

Penny paid up and added a tip. She wandered slowly home, mulling over what she'd learned.

Now she had a plan for Sunday. She needed to join the ramblers' group and get to know this Edwin Montgomery a little better. She'd seen a poster in the window of the mini-market, and it even said that dogs were welcome.

Then she pictured Kali in the midst of walkers and other dogs.

She'd go alone.

CHAPTER EIGHT

Penny had a lazy Saturday. Finally, it felt like a treat to sit around and relax – like she really was enjoying a proper life-changing retirement. She did some more sketches of her back garden, and some of Kali when she stayed still for long enough, and she was pleasantly pleased with the results. She pottered into Lincoln at one point and bought some new drawing pencils, and joined the library so she could take out some books on dog behaviour and body language. She also arranged for an extravagant hamper of wine and chocolates to be delivered to Francine.

Late on Saturday evening she took Kali for an extra-long walk, and on Sunday morning she rose early just to give the dog a chance to stretch her legs and do her business. She still felt a little guilty as she closed the front door and left Kali alone while she went off to join the ramblers' group.

It would be lovely to take her dog along. One day, she promised herself. One day soon I'll be the owner that you deserve.

The ramblers met in the car park to the south of the town. She followed the road over the old bridge and towards the Spinney. The car parking area was between the trees and the town, and it led out onto grassed land. There was the town's war memorial with its list of local names, and a children's play area. Spring bulbs were making the green grass bright with colour. Beyond the swings and roundabouts was the Slipe, the meadow land beside the river.

Penny counted nine people as she approached the car park. They were dressed in brown, green and blue, except for one very round woman who had decided to accent her size with a bright red and white polka dotted jacket, and she looked utterly fabulous.

Everyone, including polka-dot-woman, was wearing serious-looking boots and gaiters, and a few happy dogs bounded around. Penny was jealous immediately. She wanted Kali to have that kind of fun.

She recognised Ed, but he was deep in earnest conversation with another man who was clothed entirely in beige, making him look older than he probably was. The amazingly-dressed polka dot woman approached her with a smile.

"Now then! Hi, there! You're new! I'm Sheila."

"Hi. I'm Penny." She went through the usual rigmarole of explaining who she was, where she came from, and why she'd moved to Upper Glenfield. She noticed that everyone around them was listening in. She didn't mind. It would hopefully save her from having to repeat herself later.

Ed nodded to her as he gathered the group around him, and began to outline where they would be walking that day.

And then they were off, heading in twos and threes away from the car park and along a bridleway. Sheila kept her company, chattering about birds and pesticides and Lincolnshire's long history which seemed to involve hiding in marshes quite frequently, something about a rebel called Hereward, and an awful lot about bombers in world war two.

There was an over-excited cocker spaniel getting under

everyone's feet, and Penny couldn't work out who he belonged to. Sheila laughed as he did three circuits of the whole group, barked at a tree and tried to get under a hedge, re-emerging backwards covered in twigs.

"Look at him. Bless. Daft thing."

Dogs were an ideal conversation topic. Penny was starting to feel like she was a normal person again. "How sweet. Do you have any animals?"

Sheila shook her head. "This is my one day a week that I have free. I run the post office and I can't afford to employ staff for as many hours as I'd like, so I work all the time. Well, me and my husband between us. It wouldn't be fair to have a dog which we couldn't spend time with. But I love them, dogs, all animals really. I love watching them. That Growler comes out with us every week."

"Growler? Wow. The name isn't quite…"

"No, not at all!" Sheila's laugh was loud and scratchy, and infectious. "He ought to be called Slobberer or Daft-As-A-Brush or something. How about you? Do you have any pets?"

"I've got a new dog from the rescue centre up the road." She felt a pang of sadness. "I wish she were here.

128

But she hates other dogs and it's a lot more difficult than I'd expected. I might have made a terrible mistake taking her on." The sadness deepened. Admitting failure hurt.

"Oh dear. That does sound awkward. You can train her, though,' can't you? Don't believe that nonsense about old dogs and new tricks. They can all learn, can't they?"

"I hope so. I don't know."

A man a little way ahead of them dropped back and introduced himself as Kevin and the owner of Growler. "I hope you don't mind me butting in…"

"Please, go ahead."

"You wouldn't think so from the horrific example that my Growler is showing, there … but I do know about dogs." There followed an informative twenty minutes where Penny saw very little of the scenery but did learn an awful lot about dog training, although as Kevin advised, "Every Tom, Dick and Harry has their own opinion and let me just tell you never, ever to mention which method you think is best online unless you enjoy a nice flamewar. I have a cousin in Nottingham who no longer speaks to me because we differ on how to teach a solid recall."

"Goodness."

"Of course," he added airily, "my own opinions are entirely correct. Just so you know." He grinned and winked at her.

"Thank you so much."

Sheila came puffing up alongside them as the path widened out again. "I knew Kev would put you right."

"It's great," Penny said. "I've got so much to think about, and try. A lot of what you said about giving treats to desensitise her fear reaction is similar to what Drew said."

"Oh, Drew, the blacksmith?" Sheila said. "Nice young man. Such a shame, really, isn't it?"

"That it is," agreed Kevin.

"What's a shame?" Penny immediately imagined a dark history filled with woe and loss and possibly a mad woman in an attic, but the truth turned out to be far more prosaic, and met her existing suspicions.

"Oh, it's his blacksmithing business," Sheila explained. "I don't reckon he makes a right lot of money. He ought to move somewhere bigger and make fancy gates for rich folks."

"Mind you, it's hard for everyone," Kevin said. "Austerity and all that. People don't know how to cut back anymore, though, do they? I was reading about rationing the other day. A tiny bit of butter to last you all week. Now me, I'd use that in one go on a slice of toast and think nothing of it."

"True, true," Sheila said.

"He's doing field-craft courses now, though, isn't he?" Penny said. "He seems enthusiastic about that."

"Well, that's dependent on folks at the conference centre, isn't it?" Kevin said. "And they are odd folks. City folks. It's all very well in the summer, I suppose. Very hit and miss, you mark my words."

Penny got the impression that they didn't consider field-craft to be a "proper" job, unlike blacksmithing which was all macho and tradesmanlike.

They tramped along a bridleway, easily wide enough for four people abreast. The group was strung out and straggling, and the pace was noticeably slower. Penny had brought a cheese sandwich with her and she was starting to think of it with longing. Her stomach growled.

"Now, take that Mary, for instance," Kevin said. "If we're talking money problems and so on. Have you heard about what happened to her car?"

"Now then, Kevin!" Sheila said. "You dreadful gossip! But go on, no, I haven't heard…"

Penny listened eagerly to the conversation between Sheila and Kevin.

"Repossessed, it was," Kevin said. "Her car, not her house. Gone!"

Sheila gasped dramatically. "Never!"

"True as I stand here. I saw them turn up and take it away on a big old lorry. She must have got one of them log-book loans since losing her job and everything. Sharks, they are."

"Oh my. How awful!" Sheila's voice had lost the edge of glee and she sounded genuinely concerned. "Now what will she do? Lost her fella, lost her job, lost her car…"

"It's a rum business all round. Still," Kevin said, "it's not like she was any good at her job. Any of her jobs. She was lucky to keep that last one as long as she did, what with her…"

"The exact same thing we're doing now," Sheila said, and brought the conversation to a firm close. "Now then. Ed. Ed! Where's this pub we're supposed to be stopping at? My stomach thinks my throat's been cut, it does."

Ed dropped back to join them. The group was fluid, and the smaller pockets broke and reformed as they went along. Kevin fell away with Growler, and Sheila went forward to talk with another woman who was carrying some hefty and technical-looking walking poles.

"How are you finding it? Do you do much walking?" Ed asked Penny. Outside, he didn't seem as out of place as he had done in Agatha's salon. His green army combat jacket was ragged and his corduroy trousers looked battered and comfortable. She imagined he was the sort of person who would dash out to sleep in a snow hole in winter, just because he could.

"I'm enjoying it," she said with honesty. "I've been walking more these past few weeks anyway, and it's a good way to get to know the area."

"Great."

They walked in silence for a while and she searched around for an opener to a profitable conversation. Eventually she said, "So, you're an electrician?"

"Mm. A bit. I can't do bathrooms. That needs a separate certificate which I don't have. I do general household maintenance. Have you something needs doing?

If I can't do it, I can always put you in touch with someone who can help you."

"I've just moved in so I might have," she said vaguely. In truth, the cottage was in perfect condition. She considered breaking something so she'd have an excuse to get him to come over. But then what? Was she going to just ask him outright if he had killed David? No. She had to be more subtle. Tact, she told herself. I need to start learning it. What would Miss Marple do?

They were climbing up to a ridge and they joined a narrow single-track road. "Where are we?" she asked as they stomped along the ridged and patched tarmac.

"Heading towards the pub," he said, loud enough for Sheila to hear. She whooped in reply.

"Whose land is all this?"

"That to the left is farmed by Dawson for a massive agribusiness based the other side of Lincoln. Down to the right ... well, that's Hart's land." Ed's pace picked up and he shoved his hands into his jacket pockets. Penny scurried to keep up, choosing to ignore the obvious body language that he didn't want to talk any more. Tact? There was a time and a place for it, and she decided now was not that time.

"Oh yes," she said innocently. "That poor farmer who died."

"Poor farmer?" Ed hissed. He didn't look at her. "*Poor farmer?* People like that don't value their place as stewards of the land. It's all money, to them. Nothing but profits. Rip up the hedges and grow more crops. Kill all the wildlife with pesticides and monoculture. Last year, when I was …" He coughed and stamped hard on the ground. "Before here, I was in a place where there was a farmer just like him. Destroyed the land, he did. Fields with no boundaries, crop dusting by aeroplane, hundreds of acres and he only employed one man because it was so industrialised."

"Where was that? It sounds awful."

Ed growled. "Nowhere. There's the pub up ahead." He surged in front of her, trying to shake her off.

Penny thought, how rude! It's not just me that needs to learn some politeness. She was determined not to let him get away from her. She stretched her legs to catch him up, but misjudged the ragged edge of the road where it met the scrubby grass, and her left ankle turned without warning, sending her tumbling to the ground with a stifled cry. She crumpled as she fell, landing on her bottom and her hip, but managed to catch her upper body with her outstretched arm.

"Ouch! Oh, blazes–"

Ed half-turned his head for a moment, but he kept on going, not even slowing down. Sheila and another woman were at her side instantly, leaning over her, and the rest of the group that were coming up behind soon gathered around. Everyone was asking if she was okay.

"My ankle..." It was red hot with bright pain.

Someone, a random man, pushed forward and knelt down to probe her leg. "Let's get you to the pub, and strap you up," he said. "There's no bone sticking out and you probably won't die. Likely it's a strain. Come on, folks."

She was lifted up by the kindness and strength of strangers and they carried her aloft to the pub. There was no sign of Ed ahead of them.

"He'll have gone to organise some ice," Sheila said charitably, and to Penny's surprise, when they got to the pub she saw that Sheila was proved to be correct.

She became the centre of attention in the cosy village pub, and she didn't particularly like it. It was one of those "I'm too English for my own good" places with a general theme of polished dark wood and horse brasses. She was installed on a padded bench seat, all deep red velour, and generally fussed over. Her sandwiches lay uneaten in her small rucksack, and instead everyone ordered enormous plates of chips with three token lettuce leaves called "salad" and a lot of different sauces.

One of the ramblers, the man who had probed her ankle when she'd first fallen, declared he had some medical knowledge and the others didn't stop him or correct him, so Penny had to trust it was okay to let him take her boot off and have a good feel. He declared it thoroughly sprained and prescribed ice, elevation and rest.

It was clear she wouldn't be continuing on the walk.

"Just let me call a taxi," she said but Sheila was already on the phone to her husband, insisting that he drag himself away from the television. She ordered him to drive over and collect them both. "He can catch up with the sport anytime. My new boots are giving me blisters anyway," she said to Penny. "You're a wonderful excuse for me to go home."

It was probably a lie but the deed was done. Penny had no choice but to sit in state, or at least sit in *a* state, her leg up on a stool, while people ferried drinks to her and reminisced about their own walking injuries. The tales grew more and more gruesome as the extended lunch hour dragged on. Penny remembered a time in Bolivia when she'd witnessed someone fracture an ankle. She kept it to herself. Her own ankle pain was putting her in a slightly bad mood.

Sheila's husband turned out to be a man as small and round as she was, and though he glowered at his wife, he smiled warmly to Penny. The ramblers helped her out to the battered blue Volvo in the car park, and she was waved off as if she had been their long-lost friend.

"Now then," Sheila said, patting her knee. They were both sitting in the back. "Have you got everything you need? Shall we call for some milk? Aspirin? Vodka? Bread? Gin? I'd recommend gin, personally. Do you want any…"

"I'm fine, I'm fine." In truth she was weary, and her ankle was throbbing, and she simply wanted a hot bath and some painkillers. And maybe a gin and tonic, later on.

Sheila's husband helped her from the car to her front door; they could hear Kali attempting to bite her way through the wood and she winced in embarrassment. Sheila reminded her of Kevin's help, and she promised to look after herself and the dog. The leave-taking was protracted and Penny was silently screaming for them to go.

Yet when she flopped down on her sofa in relief, painkillers ready and a gin on the table, a switch flicked on in her head. Now she was alone, Kali leaning against her, she could properly think about what she'd learned on the walk – apart from the lesson that she needed to take more care.

She reached out for her mobile phone and called Cath.

* * * *

"No, you're not disturbing me. The kids are playing computer games and I'm just looking at some gardening magazines," Cath said.

"Are you a keen gardener?" Penny thought about her increasingly muddy back yard, with added holes courtesy of the dog.

"I'm a total dreamer, nothing more. I've got kids, remember. I fantasise about decking. What I've got is a wasteland and a broken football goal. Anyway, what can I do for you?"

"I've got news about the case. I'm sure it's Edwin Montgomery. He's the murderer."

There was a silence. Penny waited, scratching behind Kali's ear. The dog leaned harder and began to make a strange snoring noise, but with her eyes half-open.

Finally, Cath said, "You're talking about the David Hart situation, aren't you? I may have spoken unwisely when you came to the party. Alcohol . . . is not to be trusted."

"No, not at all. I pressed you on it. It was my fault. But I feel I am involved, somehow. I did find the body, didn't I?"

"That does *not* make you involved."

"It was horrible. I've never seen a dead body before. Except that guy in Ruislip who was stuck in a cardboard box but that probably doesn't count. I want closure. Or something. Anyway, listen." She could hear herself sounding almost rude but she was so keen to get her thoughts out in the open. "I've worked it out. Ed's a prime suspect. I've met him twice now. He was really angry about landowners like David Hart. I mean, he sounded furious. I think I upset him a bit. But there's more. He's also good with electrical stuff, you see. It could be him! It *is* him!"

"Oh, Penny. I appreciate what you're trying to do, but honestly, although he was electrocuted, it can't have been the fence. It was a temporary one that ran off some batteries, remember? They've been down and checked and everything. It's confirmed. The forensics boffins have categorically stated that the fence is absolutely fine and did not have the voltage, or the amperage, or the current, or whatever it is, to kill a man. They said something about the "volts that jolts, the mills that kills", and then laughed, and said it wasn't the fence."

Penny pouted to herself. "Edwin Montgomery has a major grudge, though. Even if he didn't tamper with the fence. You said before that he *had* been electrocuted. So maybe Ed had some way of doing that…"

"You do know that electricians don't carry the electricity around with them, don't you?"

Ouch. Penny closed her eyes briefly and before she could reply, Cath continued, saying hastily, "I'm sorry. That was uncalled-for. I'm just concerned that you're getting too … involved. You can leave it to the professionals. To us."

Penny's ankle throbbed. Kali made a growling sound

but her face was relaxed and her tail wagged. Maybe it was the painkillers, but Penny felt a laugh bubbling up inside her at the image of an electrician supplying his own power out of a toolbox – tadaah! – like a superhero, lightning bolts springing out when he opened the lid. "No, I did call for it, and you're right, and it's funny. I'm sorry. I have had a bad day. And a good one, in ways. Oh goodness. I'm getting delirious. Hang on." She took a deep breath. She hadn't had *that* many painkillers. Maybe it was the gin, too. "Right. You can't deny that Ed had a motive, though, right?"

Cath tutted but it did sound as if she were smiling. "Maybe he did. We shouldn't even be talking about this. So yeah, he did have motive. And I'm only saying this to get you to stop meddling but we did call him in for questioning."

"You arrested him! Why is he still out and about then?"

"No, he was not arrested. He was on the list of suspects so they called him in to ask some questions, and he came voluntarily. He …" Cath dropped her voice. "He has a record for industrial sabotage, which sounds very fancy but it could just be as simply as cutting a hole in a fence."

"There, you see! Motive and previous form!" Penny sat bolt upright, startling Kali who slid to the floor with a thump and remained there, grumbling.

"Yes. And no. Mostly, no. The inspector let him go, and said he was no longer to be considered as part of the investigation. I was in the office. Open plan offices are great. Someone queried it and he was told to shut up and not mention it again."

"Wow. What does that mean?" It sounded deliciously dodgy to Penny.

"I don't know. Probably nothing. The main thing is, Penny, that Edwin Montgomery is not a suspect in this case. He is innocent."

"But—"

"I've got to go. One of the kids is *alleged* to have jammed the other kid in a cupboard. I don't believe it. But I've got to go… Sorry. And look, please, you're going to get into bother if you focus on this. *We'll* catch the killer. You don't need to worry. It looks like a targeted attack, not some random indiscriminate murder. Upper Glenfield is quite safe."

"I'm not—"

There was muffled shouting on the other end of the line. Cath hollered something at her children then returned to the conversation. "Look after yourself. Maybe we could do coffee some time? Wait – no! Put that down! Put *him* down. Look, I've got to…"

"Yes, yes, of course. Thanks."

Penny let her mobile drop to the cushion beside her. So, not only was Ed not a suspect, he was not to be thought about, spoken about or anything?

There was something *very* strange going on in Upper Glenfield.

CHAPTER TEN

Penny wondered if her house was beginning to smell. She might not be able to tell, if she got used to it. She hadn't done much housework since the ankle sprain, and she hadn't left the cottage either. After all, the doctor had recommended that she rest. Now it was Wednesday, and Kali was practically eating the wallpaper off the walls with cooped-up craziness, and Penny knew exactly how she felt.

She lay on the sofa and flicked through the television channels. It all seemed to be house auctions, women's makeovers, and some terrible documentary about barnacles. Doing nothing was both tiring and frustrating. Her eyelids began to droop again. The less she did, the more she wanted to sleep. Was she actually beginning to hibernate? Could humans even do that?

Kali began barking a fraction of a second before the

knock at the door. Penny startled awake and sat up, unsure whether she had heard the knock or dreamed it. It came again, and she made her way to answer it. Her ankle was sore but the three days of inactivity were helping a lot to ease the pain and accelerate the healing process.

It was Drew, and she was pleased to see him, in spite of his dire warnings against asking questions. "Hi there," he said cheerfully. "I just thought I'd call round to see how you were getting on with the head-collar and Kali."

Kali was alternating between pressing herself against him and sitting back, squashing herself down on her haunches and making a strange bubbling throaty noise – the same over-excited reaction she showed just before getting fed. Drew bent and petted her, and noticed the bandage around Penny's ankle. She was in loose linen trousers and was barefoot.

"Oh – are you all right?" He straightened up, his fingers lightly resting on Kali's head. She grumbled happily.

"Yes," Penny replied. "This, oh, it's nothing. I sprained my ankle at the weekend, that's all. Come in."

"Of course, sorry. You need to sit down."

"It's not so bad now," she said over her shoulder as

she led him into the kitchen, defaulting to the usual 'I have a visitor so I must put the kettle on' routine. "I can walk better on it today."

"When did you do it? Down, Kali!"

"On Sunday. I went out with the ramblers."

"Sunday! My goodness. How have you been managing? Have you seen a doctor?"

"Yes, on Monday, and that was very interesting. I've got a lot of questions about…" but she tailed off as she caught his guarded expression, and remembered that he had advised her to stay clear of the investigation.

But it was no use. She was bubbling with speculation and she'd been housebound for three day with nothing to occupy her thoughts.

Drew knelt to give Kali more fuss. "I'm glad you saw a doctor. What about Kali? How have you been walking her? I know there's a dog walking service in Lincoln. Did they come out?"

"Is there? I didn't think of that. Huh. It will be six weeks before they can connect my internet, apparently. An engineer has to come out and put a phone line in. Who on earth lives without a phone line?" Penny poured the boiling water into two mugs. "I've let her out into the back garden to do her business and I've been throwing a ball for her, but I haven't been able to take her out. On the plus side, though, I've taught her some tricks. And I've been learning from some books I got from the library."

Drew looked furious. "She hasn't had a walk for three days? That's insane. That's awful. The poor dog! Why didn't you call me?" He rose to his feet and Penny felt suddenly guilty.

"I didn't have your number…" she stammered.

"You could have … oh. I see. Okay." He sighed. "I'm sorry."

"No, it's all right. You're totally correct. She does need some exercise."

"Well, that's settled." He beamed. "After my cuppa, I'll take her for a walk. No arguing."

"I won't argue. That would be lovely, thank you."

"And here's my number in case you do need it." He pulled out an envelope from his pocket and tore off a corner, and she passed him a pen to scribble with. "It must be strange, being here all alone in a new place."

"I like it. Or I did like it, up until when I needed people

and realised I didn't have anyone."

"Your London friends not beating a path to your door, then?"

"I don't think I have any London friends," she confessed sadly. "It's been really obvious that the one person I made any emotional impression on was Francine. No one else has stayed in touch at all. You remember…?"

"Yes, she came to see you."

"Yeah." She laughed. "Everyone else, though, has stayed away. No phone calls, nothing. I suppose it would have been different if I'd moved to the Cotswolds. It's trendy there."

"Why didn't you move to somewhere trendy? I mean, much as I love Lincolnshire, why come here? People generally … don't."

Penny thought it was a strange question coming from someone so obviously rooted in the area. "I came here partly because I wanted to be far away from anywhere else. And partly because the sale of my London home was pretty good but I would only have been able to afford a shed in the Cotswolds, but here, I bought this cottage and my motorbike and I can live nicely for at least a little while."

"I see. So, you said the appointment at the doctor's was interesting…"

She drank her tea while she tried to come up with something to say. She failed.

Drew smiled thinly. "You're still poking into that business with David Hart, aren't you? I saw in the paper that it said he'd been electrocuted and the death was being treated as suspicious. So everyone's talking about it."

"Yes," she said, all her fire and passion coming back in a rush. He had brought the subject up, so she decided it was fair game again. She sat forward, wrapping her hands around her mug. "Can you confirm for me something about Mary, David's girlfriend? Did she use to work at the surgery?"

Drew tipped his head back and studied the ceiling. "Yes, she did. But not for very long, I don't think. I don't go to the doctor much. All the healthy outdoor air, you see. I'm of hardy stock."

She didn't look at his wide shoulders. "Right, that's fine, I just wanted to know that it was the same Mary. She seems to have a reputation for not sticking at jobs. What is up with her?"

"Nothing." He lowered his gaze. "Nothing as far as I know, but I don't know her."

"I thought everyone knew everyone in a small town," she teased. "You said you knew my business. You knew about Francine coming to stay."

Drew shrugged again. "Yes and no. Honestly, I try to stay out of the gossipy stuff. It's easier."

No, she thought, I reckon you've been taking an interest in ... me. Huh. She pushed the thought aside. It wasn't entirely unwelcome but it wasn't quite comfortable. She said, "So you won't have heard that Mary's car has been repossessed? She's having money troubles, apparently."

"That's a shame," he said, with a look of empathy on his face. "I know what it's like. She's not on your list of suspects, is she?"

"Not at the top, no."

"Who is at the top? Not that I am interested or condone your meddling in any way," he added hastily, with a forced frown that was utterly unconvincing.

Aha! She thought in triumph. You're snared, just like me. And everyone else. "I don't know. Edwin Montgomery was a suspect but I have heard that he has been questioned and the police have completely taken him out of their enquiries. And that's very odd because he does have a history of sabotage *and* he's an electrician *and* he has a motive because he hates farmers and he particularly hated David Hart. So…"

"He must have an alibi then. They will have a time of death by now. I trust the police to sort it out. As should you."

"I wish I could get my hands on the facts that the police have!" she said in frustration.

"Why? Do you think you could do better? They have expertise and technology and experience."

"Yes, but I have an enquiring mind," she insisted. "That counts for something, right?"

She could tell from the expression on his face that it counted for very little. He said, "Don't let it get to you."

She had never told him exactly why she had felt she had to leave London. The truth was, that she had let many things "get to her" and it had started to affect her life, both personally and professionally. Not that she had had much of a personal life.

The stress had started to do things to her mind, and

her body. The blood pressure, the headaches, the dizzy spells, and strange mood swings. She decided to keep it to herself.

She wasn't ashamed – not exactly – but the person she'd been, the past few years, wasn't the "real" Penny. She'd become something else.

She was here in Upper Glenfield to reclaim the real Penny. That was the only Penny that she wanted Drew to see.

Not that she wanted or needed to impress Drew, though, she reminded herself sternly. All it was … all it was … she just didn't want him to think she was a bit pathetic, that was all.

She felt the negative thought and stamped on it. *Not* pathetic. Just … lost.

"Are you okay?" he asked in concern.

"Yes, fine. I'm just thinking. I know that David's brother Thomas lives with his wife Eleanor here in Upper Glenfield."

"You have done a lot of investigating!" He folded his arms in mock annoyance. She thought it was mock, at any rate.

"No, I just went to have my hair done at Agatha's salon. I didn't meddle. Information happened to come to me while I was being styled."

Drew looked embarrassed but she interrupted him before he could say anything. "No, don't tell me that my hair looks nice, because I know you didn't notice, and it wasn't really a drastic enough style that anyone should notice."

"Sorry. You would have thought my mum would have trained me better."

Penny laughed at his contrite expression. "Anyway. So were, or are, Eleanor and Mary good friends?"

Drew shook his head. "I have no idea, seriously. I don't know Eleanor at all, and I only know Mary by sight. And reputation."

"Ugh. I was hoping you'd have great insight."

"Sorry. Can I make it up to you by walking Kali, instead?"

"Oh, go on then."

"Cheers."

She watched him leave, the dog by his side, and felt funny. It was a domestic sort of scene and one that was unfamiliar to her in so many ways.

* * * *

Some pixies or goblins had broken in overnight and healed her ankle. When Penny woke up on Thursday morning, she felt miraculously better. Enforced rest had finally done the trick. She strapped her ankle up carefully, but by lunchtime she felt bold enough to take Kali for a walk. She was armed with lots of chopped ham and the head-collar.

She still went straight for the lonelier paths, however, rather than chancing the busy town centre. She followed what she remembered of the route she'd taken on Sunday with the ramblers. She made Kali walk to heel while they were on the pavement and the road, with sudden turns and stops and waits to keep the dog focused. Once they were on the bridleway, Penny slackened off the lead and Kali plunged into the vegetation at the side, her tail thrashing from side to side as she was inundated by thousands of scents and smells.

It's Facebook for dogs, Penny thought as Kali spent

forty seconds sniffing a small patch of grass. There's some dog's status update there, all conveyed through the pungent medium of pee. Eww.

She kept an eye out for other walkers. Another person meant potentially other dogs, and many would let theirs off-lead. She didn't quite know what she'd do if another dog came running at Kali. Would she still be able to hold her back with the head-collar? She felt hot and anxious as she replayed some disaster scenes in her head.

"Leave it!" she said out loud, and Kali stopped and looked up at her, her brow furrowed.

"Sorry," she said to the dog. "I meant me, not you."

They walked on. The edges of this section of the bridleway were bordered on the left by an impressive hedge, and on the right by a wooden fence. The hedge grew taller and thicker as they went along, and the bridleway up ahead curved around to the left, snaking behind the bushes and shrubs.

She was always nervous when approaching a part of the path where visibility was reduced. She slowed, and Kali seemed to feel the tension travel down the lead, because her ears flattened and her eyes rolled.

Penny realised that she was making the dog more reactive. She took a deep breath and relaxed her grip on the lead. "Come on, girl," she said in an artificially cheery voice.

Of course, it was then inevitable that as she rounded the corner, she would be faced with someone coming the opposite way. She hauled on the lead in panic, which meant Kali lunged forward eagerly.

But it was only Ed, and he had no dog. Her hot fear turned to a wash of relief that felt like cold sweat on her back.

"Hi, Penny," he said. "Oh! What a lovely dog."

It still amused her that having a dog was such a conversation starter with people. And it made a refreshing change from the usual conversation that inevitably followed: "aargh, a Rottweiler!" She smiled, and said, "Thank you. This is Kali. She's a bit bad-mannered," she added in apology as Kali pressed right up to Ed, stopping just short of planting her muddy paws on his legs.

"No, she's adorable! You could have brought her with you on our walk last Sunday. How's your ankle, by the way? It's good to see you up and about."

He spoke to the dog, rather than to her. She said, "It's

a lot better but I've spent the last few days just lying on my sofa. This is the first time I've been out on it, properly."

"I'm glad to hear you're better. It was a nasty tumble. I hope it hasn't put you off."

"No, not at all. I will certainly come again." She marvelled at the ice-breaking properties of Kali. The previous encounter between them had been wiped away; Ed was talking with her quite sociably. Albeit without looking at her.

"Excellent," he said.

She felt bolder now she had Kali with her, and Ed seemed quite approachable. She took a breath and plunged in. She decided she would simply confront him straight out. "David Hart was electrocuted to death, and you're an electrician who didn't like him. And I know you were questioned by police and released. I'm really curious, though. You're not a suspect and that's great. But…"

Oh. Oh no. She could hear what she was saying as if from a great distance away, and it was all wrong. She would have crammed the words back into her mouth if she could. Ed stopped petting Kali, and rose to his feet, his fists clenched. Kali picked up on the tension in his body and retreated to Penny, sitting on her foot and facing Ed, a low growl warning him to stay away.

"Do *you* think I killed him?" he asked in a low voice.

"I – er, obviously not, because, er, yeah, so I wouldn't ask a killer if he is a killer when we were out alone in the countryside because that would be stupid," she gabbled, thinking, I am *so* stupid. I am the Queen of Stupid.

"And hang on one minute," Ed continued. "How did you know I'd been questioned? That's a breach of trust. Who told you?"

"No one. I mean, I've been really nosey and I'm sorry and I shouldn't have and…" And don't kill me, she added privately.

Ed's face was ashen white, and his fists were blotchy, hanging by his sides. He half-turned away, his lips in a snarl.

Then he sagged at the shoulders and kicked at the ground, like a sulky teenager. "You're just the sort of person with time on their hands and a sense of entitlement that you won't let it go, will you? You'll dig and dig. So let me save you some time. Yeah, they took me for questioning. Of course they did. I have a record, don't I? I'm constantly being punished for believing that the Earth deserves better care than we give it. Whatever." He swore under his breath. "The thing is … I was involved in a group and we were really passionate about what we did. We believed that we *had* to act to make things better. And you know what? I still believe that."

She didn't dare speak even though he had paused to glare at her. She nodded slowly.

"Right," Ed said. "But this group went too far. Now me, I believe all life is sacred. *All* life," he said meaningfully. "I wouldn't take a life. But the others, they had a hierarchy and they thought that we were literally in a war, and that in a war, it was okay if people got hurt. Or worse."

"So what happened…?"

Ed started to pace around them. Kali watched him warily. "I turned grass. I became an informer. I fed information back to the authorities because although I believed in the group's aims, I hated their methods."

"Oh my goodness." He really was some kind of eco-warrior, she thought.

He stopped abruptly, right by her shoulder, and whispered, "And that's why I'm here, all right? I'm lying low because right now, people are in prison because of me.

And I'd really rather you didn't gossip about *that*, thank you very much."

She took a step back, gaping at him. "I won't. I promise."

He raised an eyebrow. "You promise? I don't know you. I don't know if your promise means anything."

"I feel awful. I am so sorry. It does mean something."

"You feel awful? Tough luck. You went digging in things you didn't ought to have dug in, so I don't care if you feel awful or not. I do care if you end up blabbing and putting my life in danger."

"I won't. I absolutely won't. I respect you. Is there anything I can do?"

He started to walk away, but called back over his shoulder. "Yeah. Keep your mouth *shut*."

She would.

* * * *

Penny walked back to her cottage feeling thoroughly chastened. Kali picked up on it through her body language, and mirrored it in her own, slouching along with her head held low and the lead slack between them.

She longed to tell Cath what she'd learned about Ed. After all, Cath was curious about why he'd been so summarily dropped from the list of suspects. Now Penny knew, and she couldn't share it with Cath. And that felt like she was betraying Cath's confidence in her.

And did she have a duty to share it with the detective constable? But if Cath's superiors did not see fit to share the details with the others, then Penny didn't have the right, either.

It was a mess. Drew had been right. She should stay out of it all. Now she understood what he meant about it being easier if you kept yourself to yourself.

She let herself into her cottage and unsnapped the lead. Kali bounded through to the kitchen and a moment later, Penny heard her lapping at her water bowl. Penny remained in the hallway, still wearing her coat and boots.

The cottage was quiet. Quiet and empty.

The more she dealt with other people, the more she realised she was alone. For a second, she wondered if the answer was to simply become a complete hermit.

No, that was nonsense. She bent to unlace her boots

and thought about Ed, though her memory of the encounter made her bristle with shame. She really had acted like a twit. He was an admirable character, in spite of his oddities. Penny tried to imagine being so passionate about the environment that she would join a group and fight for it.

It was a great idea but such a commitment, and she was lazy. She knew it. Most people were. Ed's drive was inspiring.

There were smaller ways to give back to the community or the land, she thought. All I do is take. I need to get involved in things and that way I'll be a positive member of society *and* I'll meet more people. The ramblers' group is just the start. Maybe there is a litter-picking group somewhere. Or I could go on those weekends where you learn hedge-laying. Or volunteer somewhere. A soup kitchen, perhaps?

Are there homeless people in the countryside? To her shame, she realised she didn't know.

There's poverty, though, she thought. I've seen that. The thin people who wait for the clearance food to be marked down in the mini-market. Little signs. She prised her boots off and dumped her jacket on the post at the bottom of the stairs.

She thought again about the murder case. If I get to know people and get involved in a properly altruistic way, then they will be more likely to open up to me, and I can find David Hart's murderer! She then thought that her motives might not be entirely altruistic. Did that matter? It was all about the end result, after all.

Perhaps. Something niggled at her, something in the conversation she'd had with Ed, something about action and end results.

Something important.

She pushed it out of her mind as Kali padded back through to see why she was still standing in the hallway.

"I'm coming," she told the dog.

She went to the kitchen and looked at the mess of paperwork on the kitchen table. She'd drawn up a list of suspects while she'd been bored and inactive. She believed Ed and what he said about his history, but wasn't going to be too hasty and take him completely off the list. She just moved him to the bottom.

This put Thomas Hart, the estranged brother, right at

the top.

I need to find out about him, she thought. So that means I need to make friends with his wife, Eleanor. And probably her friend Mary, too. Everyone's been pretty disparaging about Eleanor's snootiness, so Mary might be the easier woman to get to know.

And that will allay any suspicion about my motives, too, she thought in triumph. It will look more natural if I become friends with Mary and then Eleanor, rather than going straight at Thomas – like I did with Ed.

And I know just how I can meet up with Mary. I know exactly where she is likely to be, socially.

She felt quite pleased with herself then.

"See," she told the dog. "I'm learning, aren't I?"

CHAPTER ELEVEN

On Friday afternoon, Penny gathered up her sketches and her watercolours, and stacked them neatly in a newly-purchased portfolio case. Kali watched her from a corner of the living room.

"Don't you start as well," Penny said. The dog's expression was almost reproachful. Penny knew she was projecting her own internal doubts onto her, but even so, it was unsettling.

Kali licked her lips and turned away.

Penny sighed and tucked a tin of pencils into the outside pocket of the portfolio case. When she'd got back from the morning walk, her mobile phone had been ringing from where she'd left it on the table in the kitchen; it had been Francine.

Francine had sounded delighted that Penny was off to

the local craft group in the community hall.

"Do you know anyone there?" Francine asked.

"No. I saw the poster in the mini-market. I hope to meet Mary and ... oh, well, you know. New people."

Francine was immediately suspicious of Penny's motives. "Who is Mary?"

"Just someone I'd like to get to know better..."

"Oooh!" Francine squealed in excitement. "You're prying into the murder thing, aren't you? Have they not found anyone yet?"

"No. And I'm not prying. I'm a concerned citizen. And I'm just trying to make friends."

"How exciting! Is Mary a suspect? Who was she, in relation to the farmer?"

Penny was torn between wanting to share her suspicions with someone who was interested, and wanting to keep it private and her own little secret. "She was his girlfriend. Look, I do have to go ..."

"Phone me later! Tell me everything! And thank you for the hamper. You shouldn't have."

"It was nothing. Okay, okay, I will call you, okay."

Penny turned her phone to silent and shoved it into

her pocket. Francine's exuberance did make her smile. Would Penny be as keen to pursue the murderer if Francine hadn't encouraged her?

She was certainly helping Penny to reclaim her lost youth.

She put her musing aside. She had a mission! "I'm off now," she told Kali. "You be good."

* * * *

The community hall was a long, low building on the east side of town, on Back Street which ran behind the church. At the end of Back Street the road turned at a funny angle to follow along the river. Opposite to the river were three long straight roads, with a late 1900s look about the rows of terraces. It was the sort of scene that needed cobbles on the street and washing strung across from house to house, rather than shiny new cars and satellite dishes.

Inside the community hall, there was a buzz of activity. It smelled like all village and community halls smelled – a slight whiff of damp, industrial cleaning fluids, dust and large vats of tea kept at a continual rolling simmer since the end of the war.

The usual folding tables had been set out in a horseshoe shape, and various people fussed around. Most of them were women, and they were all of a certain age. That age being the more mature side of fifty, at least. And in many cases, Penny was being charitable.

But this was no time to be ageist. After all, she was what she considered to be the "wrong" side of forty though was there a "wrong" side? It wasn't like she could put it "right." She was already the sort of woman that she remembered looking at when she was younger, and wondering if she would ever, ever get to that age. And here she was, at that age, and not a lot had changed.

Except her stress levels, her resilience, her sense of humour and her general reaction to life's difficulties, of course.

No. The person she once was *would* return, she promised herself. In fact, she already was. She lifted her head high and walked into the hall, clutching the portfolio to her chest.

She was greeted enthusiastically by everyone, and she thought she recognised a few faces though she could not place them. They were people she'd seen in town, perhaps, or maybe with the ramblers. Just the act of recognition made her feel warm and part of something.

A stately woman in a formal blue dress suit with intimidating shoulder-pads introduced herself as Ginni, the secretary of the group. "I'm not quite a leader," she said with a laugh, "but I am the closest thing, I think. I do the paperwork, which is power, of a sort."

Penny was introduced to everyone in a whirlwind round and promptly forgot all the names. All except one, the very woman she was here to talk to: Mary.

There was a spare seat either side of her, and Penny sidled onto the left side. Mary smiled warmly. She was in her early fifties, perhaps, with slightly mad fuzzy hair and enormous purple-rimmed spectacles. She was a loose-skirt-and-bangles sort of woman, with a throaty laugh.

"Penny! Now then, duck, you sit here and tell me all about yourself!"

Perfect! Penny grinned back. "I'm sorry ... so many new names. Mary...?"

"That's right, Mary Radcliffe, that's me. So you're new to Upper Glenfield, are you? What brings you here?" Mary's eyes glistened with something very like greed and Penny realised that here was a woman who collected gossip in the way that others collected stamps or coins.

She didn't look like a woman in mourning for the love of her life, either, but then, Penny reminded herself, who was she to judge? Grief – like stress – took people in different ways. She was increasingly sure that there wasn't a checklist of "things to feel when someone dies."

Penny told her a little about London and her career in the heady world of television, but Mary had a particular talent that seasoned rumour-mongers all had. She was able to tease out more information that Penny had intended on giving. It was a skill Penny wanted to learn, although not by being on the receiving end of it.

"Stress, hey?" Mary was saying. "Enough that you gave up your job and moved away? That sounds more like a breakdown to me."

Penny shook her head – nothing so dramatic – but Mary was unstoppable. She blundered on. "There was a woman that I knew, lived up on the Abbeystead estate, oh, she was terrible with it. Terrible. Made herself quite ill, you know? I saw her once, she hadn't washed her hair in two weeks, no make-up, shocking, it was!"

"That sounds more like depression," Penny hazarded, grabbing a gap in Mary's stream of words.

"Well, they do go together, don't they? As I am sure you know."

"No, I–"

Mary patted her hand. "I'm sure you're a very private person and you don't know me at all, but I want you to know you can always come to me if you need to talk. I'm a very good listener. Everyone knows."

Penny glanced around. 'Everyone' seemed very intent on their own business in their own little groups, and there was a noticeable space around the pair of them. No one looked their way.

Mary was clearly not as popular as she thought she was.

Penny desperately wanted to steer Mary away from the topic of stress and depression before she leaped to any more conclusions. Penny already recognised that denial on her part would simply strengthen Mary's convictions.

Penny unzipped her portfolio and began to pull out her sketches. She felt nervous about unveiling her work but it was a good tactic to divert Mary. It was much like throwing ham around when Kali spotted another dog. It worked.

"Oh my! What a talented artist you are!" Mary said, her hand darting in amongst the pile and sifting through them as if Penny had given her permission. Which she had not. "What a beautiful dog! I used to draw, you know, but I've moved on."

As if drawing was something you did until you could do something else. Penny decided that Mary was simply bad with her impulsive phrasing, not wilfully rude and tactless. She tried to rescue her sketches but Mary was intent upon them. "Is this your dog?"

"Yes, Kali. She's a Rottie."

"Oh, what vicious dogs they are! They'll rip your face off as soon as look at you. You wouldn't think it to look at her there, would you?" Mary said.

Now Penny was properly annoyed. You can say bad things about my drawings but not about my dog, she thought. She hadn't realised how protective she felt until that moment. "There is nothing vicious about Kali," she snapped.

Mary pursed her lips and ploughed on. "Barry Nuttall

had one of them. Not quite like this one. His dog was smaller, and chunkier. More like … well, it was a pit bull terrier. Or something like it. It looked like one of them banned dogs, anyway. Horrible thing. Anyway, it died!"

And your point is…? thought Penny, disliking Mary more and more. The plan to become friends was a regrettable one. She gritted her teeth and said, "So, what crafts do you do now? Is that decoupage?"

Mary pushed all of Penny's sketches aside with a dismissive sweep of her arm, the bangles jangling. "I've been making cards. High-class ones, obviously. Well, I'll decoup onto anything, but cards is easiest."

Decoup? Mary's grammar made Penny itchy and she wasn't usually a snob about how people spoke. It was all the aspects of Mary's demeanour that were making her uncomfortable. "May I see?" she asked, pointedly trying to demonstrate what good manners looked like.

Mary picked out one of the worst creations and presented it with pride. A fat robin had been cut out and glued onto a blue card, with golden glitter applied around the edge. Penny was unconvinced that it counted as 'decoupage.'

"I'm selling at craft fairs all over the county!" Mary told her. "This is one of my most popular designs."

"At Christmas?"

"I sold one last week."

"Wow," Penny said with genuine feeling. "They are certainly unique."

"They are very popular," Mary repeated. "Have you thought of selling at craft fairs?"

"No, it hadn't occurred to me. I'm not really good enough yet."

"Nonsense! A bit of work, a nice frame, someone will buy them. You'll improve. Although you probably want to draw a cuter dog. Do a terrier. Everyone loves terriers. A terrier in a bow. With flowers around it."

Penny resisted the urge to say something nasty about terriers being loved by her Rottie as a nice snack. "Well, quite," she said. "I'll see."

"No, you must!" Mary said. She was becoming quite insistent. "We could share a lift! Wouldn't that be nice? You wouldn't be on your own, and it's cheaper with petrol."

"Perhaps in the summer."

"There's a fair next weekend in Grantham. There's still

time to book a table there, only a fiver. It's not too far and it will give you a real taste for it!"

Absolutely not, for many reasons, not least of which she didn't want to spend too much time in Mary's company. "No, I'm afraid…"

"There is nothing to be afraid of!" Mary said, missing the point, possibly deliberately. "I'll book the table. You don't need to do anything except pick me up on Saturday morning. We'll have to leave early, of course. How big is your car?"

Hit the brakes! Hit the brakes right now, Penny screamed silently. "I can't. I'm busy at the weekend." It was a lie and she hated to tell it. "I'm sorry," she said. As if it were her fault. Aargh!

Mary frowned and her face was not pretty when her brows lowered and her frosted-pink lips puckered. "I lost my car recently," she said petulantly. "And I lost my job, and my dear, close gentleman-friend." She pulled out a tissue and dabbed at her eyes unconvincingly, an act which sent her right to the top of Penny's mental list of suspects. Who would list their boyfriend – well, 'gentleman-friend' – last?

"I'm sorry to hear that," Penny said. This was her chance, wasn't it? But how on earth did one ask for details about something so sensitive? She wanted to know, above all, if Mary was to be a beneficiary of David's will.

But she wouldn't be so upset about not having a car, then, would she?

Or maybe she would. Penny said, hesitantly, "Probate takes such a long time, doesn't it?"

"Especially when the poor dearly departed was *murdered*," Mary said in a low whisper, her hand darting out and gripping Penny's wrist. "Tragic. You'll have heard all about it, I'm sure. My poor David. It's in all the papers! Tragic, tragic. When you reach my age, my duck, you'll understand what a trial life is…"

Your age? I'm only five or ten years away. And yet it seemed like a lifetime. "I really am sorry to hear about your troubles." She was supposed to add 'if there is anything I can do' to be polite, but social convention could go swing for it. "Perhaps when the will is read…"

"Ha!" Mary hissed and sat up straight, her chin jutting up and out. "Fat lot of good that is to me now, is it?"

Penny winced. It wasn't going well, and people were

starting to look their way. She could read Mary's words in different ways. Had she experienced financial problems which led her to murder David in the hope of getting something from the will, unaware that probate would be delayed due to the circumstances of his death? Or did she know she was not a beneficiary anyway? Had David's death caused her *more* financial problems? Had he been supporting her in some way?

There were so many questions and no easy way of asking them. "Perhaps you have friends who might give you a lift next weekend," Penny said slowly. "Or relatives. David had a brother, didn't he? Maybe his wife, Eleanor..."

"Eleanor?" Mary's voice quivered. She repeated the name, louder this time. "Eleanor? What is *Eleanor* in all of this? Why would I speak to that woman?" She pushed her chair back, the legs scraping on the hall floor. "Who put you up to this? Who has been talking?"

It was a bit rich, Penny thought, for her to complain about gossip. "No one. I'm sorry. I thought..."

"Haven't I been through enough?" Mary wailed, and now everyone's eyes were upon them. She started to grab her cards and bits of paper, pulling them towards her in a mess of glitter and loose pictures, stuffing them into a carrier bag. "And now you throw that ... that ... *woman* into my face again. Her!"

Ahh. Well, this has answered one question, Penny thought miserably. Eleanor and Mary were no longer friends.

It probably was not the right time to ask when and how they had argued.

Mary slammed the final handful of awful cards into the plastic bag and punched a hole right through it, causing the paper to spill to the floor as she stood up. This prompted a fresh round of wailing, and Ginni stalked forward to take command of the situation, her kitten heels clacking ominously over the hard floor.

Penny shrunk down in her chair as the situation dissolved around her. Ginni glared at Penny, before turning to Mary and asking if she was all right, and did she need a glass of water.

"It's all too much for me!" Mary wailed. "All I wanted ..."

"There, there. It's okay." Ginni patted Mary and shot a slit-eyed death stare of warning at Penny. She began to put her sketches back into her portfolio case.

"I'm so sorry. I seem to have said the wrong thing. I

really didn't mean any harm." She really did feel awful. Mary's distress was quite genuine, but it was odd that it was only the mention of Eleanor that set her off; she had talked about David's death with perfect equanimity.

"Yes. This is a calm and peaceful group," Ginni said.

Penny tensed. "I think I'd better go. Again, I am so sorry. If there is anything I can do…"

"You've already said you won't take me to the craft fair," Mary said, pausing her sobbing for a moment to dig at her.

"It's that I can't rather than won't…"

"I still won't be able to go, will I? After all I've been through. Oh, everything is so difficult for me…"

"You've had a nasty shock," Ginni said. "It's been a trying time for you. We all understand." She angled her broad shoulder to exclude Penny from the conversation.

Penny took the hint, and left.

* * * *

She had annoyed Drew by wanting to ask questions, and now his warning was proved justified. Cath wasn't happy. Warren was, well, just Warren. Ed had been upset by her probing, and now Mary – and the whole craft group, and by extension the entire community of Upper Glenfield – were furious with her.

Only Francine was her unlikely ally.

She should stop asking questions. She knew that.

Give it up.

Quit.

I am not a quitter, she said to herself as she stamped home, unwisely given that her ankle was still sore. She felt hot and angry, and a little ashamed that she had upset so many people.

But the fact was that a man was dead. Dead, she reminded herself. So if some folks got upset, surely it was justified?

She was hazy about the ethics of it.

Penny stopped suddenly, as a new thought hit her.

She was feeling full of energy once again. Her lethargy and her unsettled ennui that had plagued her for so long was gone. She was on fire once more. She was alive.

She had made lists in her head, and organised her time, and not once had she felt overwhelmed by it all. She hadn't shied away from essential tasks. She hadn't fallen into negative thoughts or patterns of behaviour.

This, then, was progress. Her new hair style, her cottage, her motorbike, her dog, her renewal of her art skills – yes. And it was all tied up in the murder case. It gave her a purpose.

It is my investigation, she decided. I need to find out who killed David Hart for *myself* as much as anyone else. Yes. There it is, plain and simple. It's a selfish motive. At least I'm being honest.

Which is more than can be said for everyone else I've spoken to, she though sourly. There was a lot in Mary's reactions that simply didn't add up.

Mary Radcliffe was now a prime suspect.

CHAPTER TWELVE

Penny flopped onto the sofa and put her feet up on the low coffee table. Her ankle wasn't hurting, exactly, but it was letting her know that she needed to take care. Kali jumped up and lay alongside her, her head resting on Penny's thigh. Penny absently stroked her head and ears, and Kali started up with the low rumbling that she'd found quite disconcerting in the beginning. Now she simply considered it Rottweiler Purring.

She wanted someone to talk to. She could call Francine, as she had promised, but she was far away. She wanted someone there, right now, who knew about the case. Drew, or even Cath. But they both thought she was being silly to think of herself as an investigator. And Cath couldn't condone it from a professional stand-point.

And Drew was worried about her getting more

involved. After all, such things were far better left to the police.

"They don't understand," she told Kali. "Okay. So neither do you."

Kali rolled her eyes up at Penny, hopeful that the speech that she just heard as noise predicated treats. It did not.

"Everyone's grief is different but there was something not right about Mary's reaction, surely?" she mused. "Or am I reading too much into it? She's hiding something, I'm sure of it. So she was sacked from the surgery and she likes to gossip. And everyone was avoiding her at the craft group. Usually people like to have a gossip. So why isn't she more popular?"

Kali closed her eyes.

"I bet any amount of money she was sacked for gossiping. What a wonderful, terrible job for a gossip... as that man said, the surgery should have known better than to employ someone like her! She had access to the intimate details of all the people in Upper Glenfield..." Penny shuddered. "What a disaster."

"So," she continued, in spite of Kali's disinterest,

"what other trouble has her gossiping got her into?"

She decided she wouldn't be able to go back to the craft group again, which was a shame as she was enjoying her rediscovery of sketching and drawing.

"This was still a successful day," she told Kali. "I know more than I did before, so it has to count. And I'm feeling less stressed, which is the most important thing." She thought she probably ought to dig out the blood pressure monitor that she had been given. She was supposed to track her statistics but she'd found the figures too scary. Now, though, it would be interesting to see if she was really improving.

She closed her eyes and together, she and her dog began to drift into sleep.

Only to be interrupted by a tentative knock at the door. Kali leaped down and went into full-on bark-the-walls-apart mode. Penny's heart thudded and she made her way slowly to the door. Was it Mary, come to continue the argument? Or even Ginni, who had seemed like one of those pleasant country women who were built entirely from steel girders and determination? Ginni was clearly of the stock that had flown unarmed spitfires through the night from airfield to airfield in the war. No. Ginni would have hammered more loudly.

The knock came again. Penny flattened herself against the door and wished she had a spyhole or some glass in the solid wood. "Who is it?"

"It's Drew! Are you okay?"

"Sure. Hang on." She let him in and he stared at her in curiosity.

"Is everything all right?" he asked.

"Yes, why?"

"Just that you wanted to know who it was before you opened the door. Are you expecting trouble?"

"Oh … yes. No. I mean. You're not trouble. Come on in."

"What have you been up to?" he asked her, following her along the default route of front door – hallway – kitchen – kettle.

"Nothing. I'm just relaxing."

"The last time we spoke, you were asking me about Mary and Eleanor. Are you still poking around, asking questions?" Drew asked.

Oh, goodness, she thought. Since then I've talked with

Ed and found out his secret, and caused an argument at the craft group. Should I tell him any of this?

"You warned me not to poke into people's lives…" she said cautiously.

"I did. I think it could be dangerous." He leaned on the table and folded his arms. He smiled crookedly, but his eyes were serious. "Although I bet you haven't listened to me, have you? I want to tell you to stay out of it but I have the feeling you won't. You're a grown woman and can make her own decisions … but I wish you'd listen to advice from a local. Leave it well alone."

Suddenly it occurred to her that *Drew* might be a suspect. Why else would he be so keen to get her to leave it? She narrowed her eyes at him. "Do you know how to electrocute someone?"

He blurted out a laugh. "I know exactly what you're thinking! No, but I could bludgeon someone to death with a hammer. Or poison them. I'm pretty good with wild plants."

"Eww. Must you?"

"Sorry. What you've got to understand, though, Penny, is that people don't like change around here. If you want to fit in, and I am sure that you do, you have to come in slowly and let it happen bit by bit. Not blunder in and upset everyone."

"I'm not blundering," she protested, feeling her cheeks flush as she remembered the craft group. If that wasn't blundering, what was? "Not everyone dislikes change. You, perhaps…" she said, tailing off. Yes. Maybe it was Drew who didn't like change.

He shrugged. "It's not about me."

Oh, but it was. "What are you doing here, anyway? Shouldn't you be working?" She was suspicious. "Did you come to tell me to stop asking questions again? I got the message, all right?"

He averted his gaze. Something was up. "Now then, about Mary."

"What about Mary?" She knew, even as she asked it, trying to sound innocent, that the rumours must be flashing around.

"This is a small town, Penny. You can't cause uproar in the craft group without people talking, you know."

"Oh no." She pulled out a wooden chair and sank onto it. "You shouldn't listen to gossip. I think you told me that."

He raised an eyebrow. "So, do you care to tell me first-hand?"

"Look. I have been sketching and drawing, and you know it, so it made sense for me to join the craft group, okay? It was perfectly innocent."

"Mm-hm."

"And I got talking to Mary. Or she got talking to me. She was full of gossip. Why do people avoid her?"

"Because she's full of gossip, I suppose."

"People like to gossip."

"It's different with Mary," Drew said. "I can't really put my finger on it. Maybe it's the delight she takes in passing on bad news. Like it's a power thing for her? I don't know." He shrugged. "I've always avoided her. I can't help feeling that if she gossips to me about someone, then she'll happily gossip *about* me, too."

"That's true. Anyway, so I accidentally mentioned Eleanor. Totally accidentally! I knew that Mary and Eleanor were either good friends, or they used to be. And it turned out that they *used* to be. They definitely aren't friends now."

Drew rolled his eyes. "So what happened between them?"

"Aha! You see! Curiosity is a powerful thing!"

"No, no. I'm not getting drawn into this." He waved his palms in the air. "I don't want to know."

"Too late," Penny said in triumph. "You are already part of this. And I don't know what happened between them because things got out of hand and I could hardly ask, but don't you see – whatever happened, it could be important. David's lover and his sister-in-law, once good friends but now enemies... it's vital that I find out!"

"It's not vital that you find out. It's vital that you tell the police."

"They'll dismiss it as silly women being silly gossips. I think I need to talk to Eleanor."

"I hesitate to ask," Drew said, "but how are you going to do that? Find out what groups she goes to, and infiltrate them, too?"

"I have thought about that. But I need to strike while the trail is still hot. I'm going to go to her house. I've found out where she lives." In fact, she had not really thought it through until the words came tumbling out of her mouth. Oh, she thought, so that's what I'm going to do. Jolly good.

"How did you find out where she lives?"

"By asking. I knew that she lived on the Shires estate from Agatha. Finding out the house was simple. Ask anyone while you stand in a queue to buy potatoes and they'll tell you."

Drew shook his head. "You're going to turn up on her doorstep? No. I think I preferred the infiltration idea better."

"Seriously. Maybe I just need to be more upfront with people."

"You are naïve. No, you are mad."

Penny was shocked, and a little hurt. "Perhaps," she said mulishly. "Or maybe I think that being honest is the best policy. Anyway, I'm going to have my dinner and then go over. Would you like to stay for some food?"

"Dinner?" he said with a smile. "It's teatime."

"Oh, my southern ways. Seriously. It's only frozen pizza but there is enough to share."

He shook his head and looked sad. "I don't think I should. Are you dead set on going to see Eleanor?"

"I am."

"I think you are making a huge mistake."

"I know," she said.

"I'd better go."

"Drew, please…"

He sighed. "I'm sorry, Penny. I can't stand by and watch you make a fool of yourself. You worry me. If you won't listen to me, I need to go. I don't really want to be a part of this."

"You don't have to be."

He shook his head and made for the door. He looked unhappy; unwilling, almost. "If I stay, I am part of it. Think about this, okay?"

He left, and she sat very still, listening to him let himself out. Kali barked once at the door closing, then rushed back into the kitchen to lick Penny's hands.

"Who does he think he is, anyway?" Penny muttered to the dog.

* * * *

The pizza tasted like cardboard with a bit of plastic cheese smeared on the top. Penny would not let herself listen to her doubts. She ate half of the pizza anyway, and slid the rest into the fridge to keep for later. It might taste better once cold.

Then she dressed in warm, dark clothes; smart jeans, solid boots, and a zip-up fleece jacket. She fussed Kali and gave her a biscuit, and strode out into the night, though the striding lasted until the end of the street whereupon she switched to a normal walk, because of her ankle.

What exactly were the police doing with the investigation? A murder had been committed, she reminded herself. It took place over a week ago! Yet she hadn't seen increased patrols, or heard any definite news, or anything. Their forensics and their technology were all very well, but they needed to knock on doors and ask questions. If she were the police, she'd consider herself – Penny – a suspect. Part of her wanted to have been formally interviewed with a tape recording and everything, just like on the television.

She walked north, past a row of old cottages built in the warm yellow stone from a local quarry. The Shires estate was at the top end of town. First she went past the Abbeystead estate, which was one long curving road with large detached houses scattered along it. They were "executive" homes built in the 1990s for people who worked in the cities but wanted rural life. Penny had known folks who'd moved out of London but who continued to work there. They didn't get to enjoy rural life at all, unless you counted the many hours they spent in cars and trains, staring out of the window at fields.

The Shires was an older development that consisted of a series of cul-de-sacs either side of the main road. They were all named after trees. These houses weren't in the local architectural style or even in the local stone. She turned right along Oak Avenue, hunting for the right house. She knew it would be a well-kept house with a blue garage door, on the left-hand side, with a clipped lawn and a small fake wishing well out the front. According to her informant in the greengrocer's, anyway.

Her heart began to hammer and her palms went sweaty. It wasn't a panic attack, she knew. It was simply apprehension. A normal reaction to an abnormal situation, as her counsellor had told her.

And what could be more abnormal than to knock on a stranger's door to talk about a murder?

She knew she was getting carried away with it all. She stopped at the bottom of a driveway that led to a house that fitted the description perfectly. She had misled Drew when she'd said she knew where Eleanor lived. The woman she'd talked with in the greengrocer's had been clear on details but vague about the actual house number.

Still, this one fitted the bill.

She mentally rehearsed her speech a few more times. Penny had decided to disarm Eleanor with honesty.

But she was rooted to the spot. She went through her piece a few more times, but could not bring herself to walk up the driveway to the front door.

A net curtain in the bay window twitched to one side, and a pale face stared out at her. Penny's mouth went dry. She had to approach the door now, and it swung open as she reached the step.

An angular woman stood in the doorway. She had a pinched face with layers of impeccable make-up accenting her fine cheekbones and aquiline nose. Her hair was styled in artful waves around her head, and was a rich, glossy chestnut of a colour and tone not often seen on a woman of her years, although the main thing that gave her age away were the lines and loose folds on her neck and the backs of her hands.

She frowned at Penny who immediately felt dowdy and provincial. It was an amusing thought, given that she was supposed to be the sophisticated southerner. "Can I help you?" Even the woman's accent was refined, with no trace of Lincolnshire in it. Penny couldn't imagine her uttering the standard local greeting of "Now then, bor."

Penny smiled and stumbled into her prepared speech. "Hi. My name is Penny May. Are you Eleanor Hart?"

"Yes. Why? What are you selling? Didn't you see the signs? We don't purchase from door-step sellers."

"Don't worry. I'm not selling anything. I'm pleased to meet you. I ought to tell you that I found David Hart's body and I've become interested in the situation. I understand that your husband and his brother did not get along. I wondered if I might come inside and talk about that?"

Eleanor stared. Her red-lined lips opened in a perfect circle for a few seconds. She swallowed and tried to say something, but nothing came out.

Penny felt more and more foolish. This was a *stupid* idea. The Queen of Stupid reigned once more.

"Obviously I know that this is a difficult time," Penny added. Suddenly she was reminded of social convention, and indeed, common courtesy. She felt herself flush. "I'd like to say that I am sorry for your loss…"

Eleanor's eyes were wide and shocked. "How *dare* you come here," she whispered, her voice croaking.

"I do appreciate this might be a bad time. Here. I've written down my name and number, and popped my address on this card. You can get in touch if you want to talk about anything. I'm an outsider, you see. It might make things easier."

"Are you with a church? Or a cult? We're in the neighbourhood watch."

"No, nothing like that. I'm looking into the circumstances of the death, and…"

"Are you with the police? We've already spoken to the police."

"No. I don't think the police are looking in the right places. I'm merely a concerned citizen who feels that society these days has become too selfish. Wouldn't communities be better if we looked out for one another?" Penny was impressed by her sudden flight of fancy. None of that had been rehearsed and planned.

Her expansive plea was clearly lost on Eleanor. "Community? Ha! You've come to the wrong place if you're looking for community. There is nothing in Upper

Glenfield. Nothing. Just insular, in-bred gossips and tiresome meddlers. Such as yourself. Now kindly leave my property. I have nothing to say to you."

Penny held out the card with her contact details on but Eleanor stared down at it, and kept her hands by her sides. "Please," Penny persisted. "Is your husband home?"

She only meant it as a lead-in to ask if she might speak to him, but Eleanor reacted as if she was being threatened. "I don't need him here to defend myself," she hissed, stepping back into her hallway. "You need to leave. I give you fair warning that if you do not, I am quite within my rights to use force and weapons if I have to."

Weapons? What kind of arsenal did the woman have? Her manicured talons looked fairly vicious. Penny took two quick steps backwards, stumbling down the path. "You have a gun?"

Eleanor sneered. "No, but I can stun *any* intruder. Mark my words. You do not wish to find out."

Stun them? What, with cologne? "I am so sorry if I have upset–"

The door slammed shut. Penny darted forward again and pushed her card through the letterbox, then turned

around and ran down Oak Avenue as fast as her throbbing
ankle would let her.

CHAPTER THIRTEEN

Penny's mind was made up by the time she reached her cottage again. Something sinister was afoot in the house of Eleanor and Thomas Hart. So, they had weapons? Weapons that stunned? She thought of Thomas's background in the Army and his enmity with his brother. This had to be followed up – right away. She had promised to ring Francine but that could wait. This was important.

She dashed into her house, circumvented the alarmed dog, grabbed her car keys and left again. She felt a pang as she floored the accelerator; she wanted someone riding with her. She pictured Drew in the passenger seat, sharing the thrill.

But he was too nervous about too many things. She didn't need that sort of man in her life.

For a big, strong blacksmith, he sure didn't like to

embrace excitement and change.

Maybe she should have had Kali riding shotgun with her.

The oncoming glare of headlights made her blink and swerve, and forced all other thoughts out of her mind as she concentrated on driving. She knew she needed to go to the east of Lincoln and find a scrap yard; Lincoln wasn't a huge city, so she didn't imagine there would be too many choices. She was prepared to go around all of them until she found the right one.

As soon as she saw a chain fast-food restaurant, she pulled up and let the engine idle while she made use of their free wi-fi, browsing on her phone for all the metal recycling places in the Lincoln area. She scribbled a list – there were two likely ones – and punched the first postcode into her sat nav device.

"Lead on, Sat Nag," she instructed it, and followed the monotone instructions through the dark streets into a gloomy and deserted industrial estate.

She slowed as she approached the first destination. The streets here were very quiet and she felt conspicuous. Who drove around an industrial estate at night? No one with good intent, that was for sure. She parked half on the pavement and half on the road, and killed the lights.

She waited, looking around for signs of life as her eyes adjusted to the gloom. A tiny battered red Metro bunny-hopped past, and she saw an ashen-faced older man in the passenger seat. The driver was a spotty youth. She remembered learning to drive like that.

A figure crossed the road far ahead, and disappeared into bushes. Sleeping rough? Drugs deal? Some illicit assignation?

She shivered. It was time to go and find things out.

She closed the car door as quietly as she could, but it still sounded loud in the empty air. She walked briskly, as if she had purpose.

What weapons, she couldn't help thinking. A stun gun? What *was* a stun gun, really?

She stopped short, her heart hammering.

A Taser.

That had to be it, she thought in triumph. A Taser! David was electrocuted, wasn't he? People reported deaths from Tasers all the time.

Triumph temporarily over-rode her fear. It *had* to be

a Taser.

She continued on, but with more caution. If this was the scrap yard where Thomas was a night watchman, and he was the killer, and he was armed, then she had to be very careful indeed.

She came to the high, locked gates. The gates were solid metal but they were flanked by a chain-link fence and she peered through to the yard beyond. It was lit only by orange street lights and there were strange, shadowy piles that rose like mountains in the distance. Nearer to her was one of those cabins on legs that were supposed to be temporary, but judging by the state of it, it had been in place for decades. One of the windows was boarded up but the other showed light from behind more mesh.

This could be where Thomas worked, she thought. She stayed by the fence, looking in, wondering what she really wanted to see.

It looked like a horrible place to work. And she doubted that it paid very much. Yet his wife, Eleanor, oozed high standards. It wasn't going to be cheap to keep a woman like that in the manner she expected; hadn't Agatha hinted as much?

Eleanor didn't seem overly enamoured with living in Upper Glenfield, either. Thomas had been an international traveller, once; he'd been a close protection officer. That sounded super-sexy and very glamourous and attractive. Back then – yes, Penny could quite see how Eleanor would have fallen for him.

And now? Working nights here, or a scrap yard just like it?

The farm was worth a great deal of money, she thought. Was Thomas named in the will? That would certainly give him motive...

She hung onto the fence, her fingers curling around the wire as she stared and thought. She had to find out about the will. Weren't they listed somewhere? She doubted there was public access to such things but she wasn't quite sure. A public records office? Or was that just for births, marriages and deaths?

She played out a tempting scenario in her mind: she would sneak into the scrap yard (somehow, though the actual details of how she'd manage that were hazy) and enter the security cabin, which would be empty yet unlocked (again, for reasons unknown). Thomas – for she would be at the correct workplace – would have nipped off somewhere. A call of nature, perhaps. There on the desk would be a copy of the will that he just happened to be reading. At work. Like it was a normal thing to do. Then she'd take a snap of it with her smartphone and escape home, undetected. She saw it play out with the gloss of a movie.

It was a satisfying chain of events that spurred her on to making her move. Penny began to walk sideways, away from the locked gate, hunting for some gap in the fence. At the corner, she thought that she could see a bad join between two panels. She began to prise at it.

Light flared all around her, and she was disorientated until she realised it was coming from a flashlight behind her, making her own shadow loom up large in front of her face. She whipped around, which was a mistake, because now she was blinded from staring right into the torch's full beam. She pressed back against the fence and blinked rapidly.

"Who are you?" a man's voice demanded roughly, interspersed with some rich and fruity language. She'd heard it all before but it wasn't pleasant. "What are you doing here? Who are you?"

"Hi!" she said, brightly, as if she was out on an afternoon shopping. "I'm Penny. I'm ... er ... wondering if Thomas Hart works here?"

The flashlight moved to the side and was angled to the ground now, but all she could see was a dark silhouette. "It's none of anyone's business," he said.

"Ah. Are you Mr Hart?" she said hopefully.

The light was shone into her face again. She managed to get one eye shut in time. "I'm phoning the police. You're coming to the cabin to wait. You can explain to them what you're doing breaking into my – hey!"

She threw herself sideways. She gambled on the fact that he wouldn't expect her to try and break for freedom until he'd stopped speaking. Well, maybe that would have been the polite thing to do. Penny ducked low, shot to the side and ran in a zig zag across the road, hoping that the learner driver wasn't about to erratically appear and mow her down.

There was a stream of cursing behind her and stamping feet that didn't seem to be very fast. She wondered if he was allowed to leave the scrap yard unattended, like the way Warren seemed tied to his shop. She ignored her ankle's throbbing, and put on a burst of speed, reaching her car and fumbling to get in. She didn't dare look behind to see if he was still pursuing her. She slammed into gear and shot away with a painful grating of the engine. Her rear view mirror was filled with light; in fact, she could see three lights – the learner driver was back and the other light must have been Thomas's flashlight. It looked satisfyingly confusing. She kept on the accelerator until she was in the flow of traffic in the ever-busy city centre, and finally she was able to control her breathing.

She was sweaty, she was in pain, and she was tingling with excitement.

She was *alive*.

* * * *

Penny made herself a cup of tea when she got home, but left it standing on the table and grabbed a can of cider from the fridge instead. It seemed more fitting. She went to sit on her sofa, absolutely thrumming with adrenaline.

I feel part of something again, she thought in wonder. I'm dynamic. I'm righting wrongs. I wonder what the upper age limit is for joining the police force?

She was interrupted in her new fantasy of crime-fighter extraordinaire by the ringing of her mobile phone. It was Cath, and she was surprised. It was gone nine o'clock at night.

"Hi Cath! How are you?" She knew she sounded over-excited.

"I'm on duty," Cath said, and her voice was flat and dry. "This is a work-related call."

"Er … oh … I suppose I ought to call you Detective Constable Pritchard, then."

"Yes, quite. There have been some complaints made about you."

"Some?" Oh dear.

"Two. Two complaints in one night. At least you gave the complainants your name, and even your address. That saves us a little bit of investigation. I do not think you are in our top ten of cunning criminals yet."

Penny was irrationally peeved. If she was going to take up crime – which she wasn't, but just supposing – she'd be good at it. She would be in the top ten. She decided not to tell Cath her thoughts. Instead, she said, "I don't see what

Eleanor has to complain about – it was Eleanor who complained, wasn't it? I just went round for a neighbourly chat, and I left when she asked me to. Actually, I left when she threatened me with weapons, and I think that's something your murder investigation needs to take a good look at!"

"The fact is that our complainant, whose identity I shall neither confirm nor deny, felt harassed. And then the complainant's husband had an encounter with a strange woman later on. The husband called the wife and they compared notes. They are quite within their rights to now feel they are the centre of a campaign of harassment, Penny. What on earth were you thinking?"

"I was thinking about the will," Penny said. "Who is the main beneficiary? How can we find out?"

"We?"

"You. The police," she corrected, hastily. "Seriously. There is some kind of–"

"Penny!" Cath exploded. "Please. I am *on duty*. I can do what I can do, here, for you but you must listen. You are going to end up with an Anti-Social Behaviour Order at this rate. Do you really want an ASBO? I think they might send an officer round to talk with you tomorrow. Be honest and most importantly, be really, really sorry. Okay?"

"Okay. I understand."

There was a pause and a long sigh. Then, in a gentler tone of voice, Cath added, "Look, Penny. I am sorry about this. Let's do coffee soon, okay? We really should."

"Isn't that a conflict of interest?"

"No. I consider it damage limitation," Cath shot back, and ended the call.

Penny couldn't help grinning to herself. Cath was curious about what she had to say, she could tell. She was hampered because she was calling from the open plan offices.

She still considered the evening a success, ASBO or no ASBO.

CHAPTER FOURTEEN

Penny woke up on Saturday morning in an uncommonly good mood. The sun was shining and it was almost feeling summery. Warm sunshine and birdsong was an instant anti-depressant. More importantly, she felt she'd got somewhere significant in the case.

In spite of the potential for the pavements to be busy, she decided to be bold and walk Kali. She had a pocket full of high-value treats – the very yummy sort of stuff that Kali didn't get at any other time. She had her confidence and a spring in her step as she left the house, head held high.

She still didn't dare to go to the popular dog walking area along the Slipe, but she skirted the edge of it as she followed the road south.

She pondered the previous night's escapades. It was feeling like a dream already. She was utterly convinced, however, that the murderer had to be Thomas, and that Eleanor knew something. She might not know the whole truth, but she was clearly hiding something.

Penny hoped to meet with Cath soon, as a friend rather than as a police detective. She resolved to call her when she got home. Francine nagged at her, too, but she'd call her that evening, perhaps. Penny had to find out about the will, and more about David – she knew his parents had passed on, but did he have any children? She wished she was connected to the internet already, although she doubted she could just google up someone's will. Still, it was worth a try. She'd googled herself once and discovered some old photos of herself from various company websites that she had had no idea about. She'd stopped immediately before she discovered anything worse than enormous hair and ill-advised blue eyeshadow.

A man in jeans and a plaid shirt said hello to her as he walked past. Kali strained towards him, her tail and indeed her hips wagging in greeting. She seemed to think that everyone wanted to be her new best friend. One quick twitch of the lead attached to the head-collar, and she was back by Penny's side, looking up and waiting for a treat for being so good.

Penny didn't think she recognised the man, but it didn't matter. It felt good to be part of a community where people did say hello on a warm May morning.

Kali began to furtle and sniff under the hedgerows, pushing her nose further and further into the tangled undergrowth. Penny let her have a good root around, but suddenly Kali yelped, and went stiff, and tried to back out, but couldn't.

"What have you done, you daft dog?" Penny said, kneeling to see what the problem was.

The head-collar, although an amazing piece of kit, was designed for improving the dog's walking, and was not suited to being dragged through vegetation. The loop on the underside had become enmeshed with some leggy old thorns and weeds.

"Hang on ... keep still," she urged as she tried to see what the issue was. Of course Kali had no intention of keeping still and the more the dog panicked, the sicker Penny felt as she struggled to pull the head-collar free from the twisting tendrils. She could barely reach the problem, her arms stretched in amongst the scratching twigs and lower branches. "Please," she said, and her desperate voice made Kali pull back in fright, tightening the head-collar around her muzzle. She was whining and it was a sound that made Penny ache.

"Right, I've got it … hang on…" The only thing she could see to do was to unclip the head-collar while holding onto Kali's collar. But with the twigs in her face, and her hands scrabbling in the weeds, she lost her grip as soon as the head-collar slipped free of the dog, and Kali shot backwards, yelping.

Penny tugged hard on the now-unattached and dog-free head-collar, not caring if it broke as she hurtled out of the hedge and landed on her bottom on the pavement. Kali had disappeared but she could hear barking up ahead where a path led off from the road. Feeling ill with anxiety, her vision clouding at the edges as she didn't breathe deeply enough, she stumbled to her feet and lurched towards the path, calling for her dog.

The barking stopped. As she rounded the tree that marked the start of the path, she had a clear view.

There was Kali, sitting and looking up at a woman in lilac and hot pink, who was pulling something from her appliqued tote bag. Kali was wagging her tail. The treacherous animal.

The woman was Mary.

Penny leaped forward, feeling so shaky that her legs gave out and she sank to her knees as she reached Kali, burying her head in the dog's furry shoulders. "Oh my goodness…"

Kali butted upwards with her forehead and then accepted some kind of goodie from Mary. Penny took a deep breath and looked up.

"Thank you, thank you! I was so sure I was going to come around that corner and see…"

She couldn't describe what she feared. Another dog, the aftermath of a fight … she shuddered. "Thank you again."

"You're welcome. What a lovely dog. I recognise her from your drawings."

Hang on, Penny thought, you called her a vicious beast before, waiting for her chance to rip your face off. Then she decided that now was not the time to challenge Mary on that. She got to her feet, awkwardly, and untangled the head-collar. It was undamaged and Kali was happy to put it back on.

"About the other day at the craft group," Penny said. "I want to apologise properly for being so insensitive and talking about stuff that I didn't have the right to." She felt a little mealy-mouthed in her apology because she didn't totally mean it.

But Mary accepted it, making Penny feel even more of a sleaze. "It's fine, my duck. I need to say sorry to you. It's been so stressful lately that I over-react to some things. My emotions are all over the place. I cry at stupid stuff and laugh when I shouldn't laugh. I don't know if I'm coming or going."

"That's understandable," Penny said, feeling growing sympathy for the woman in spite of her general dislike. "How long had you and David been together…?"

It was a risky question, perhaps, but Penny hoped it sounded natural. And Mary answered quite normally. "Oh, as … partners, just a few months." She smiled. "Partners! That's the word nowadays. I prefer lovers. He was my gentleman-friend. But anyway. I've known him forever, of course. Through Eleanor. I'm sorry, that's a difficult subject…"

"Of course, of course. If I can help in any way…" Barring giving you a lift to the craft fair, she thought, and then felt like a horrible human being. So she said, "Perhaps when I am free I can give you a lift to the next craft fair…"

Mary's eyes lit up. "That would be wonderful! I wasn't able to get to that one this weekend," she added meaningfully. "I didn't book a table in the end. What with you being busy tomorrow… But the next one would be fantastic. I live up on Church Street, the cottages there. Number eighteen. I really would appreciate that." She sniffed and dabbed at her eyes with her sleeve. "Oh my goodness. Your kindness will set me off again."

Penny felt better that she had done the right thing at last, even if it meant Mary was now in tears. She reached out instinctively and patted Mary on the shoulder, which unleashed a flood of tears.

"I'm sorry, my duck, I'm sorry," Mary babbled.

"It's all right! You've got every right to cry," Penny said firmly. "You let it all out, now. There, there."

She glanced down to see Kali was pressed against Mary's leg and looking up at her in concern. Mary pulled out a tissue and blew her nose. "I'm just so fragile at the

225

moment," she said. "With everything."

"Of course." She'd lost her partner ... of just a few months, Penny reminded herself. She asked, cautiously, "You've lost your gentleman, uh, friend. Your job and your car, you said at the craft group. It's a lot for anyone to deal with. You're doing marvellously, under the circumstances."

But there was more. "Oh, and those blasted letters!" Mary blurted.

"What letters?" Penny felt a tingling in her stomach.

Mary's body shuddered as she fought to stifle her tears. "Oh, it's nothing. I really shouldn't take any notice of them. People can be so spiteful. I know I'm not perfect. Who is? But they send them anyway."

"Mary, let me get this straight. Someone's sending you horrible letters?" That was low. That was lower than low. Poor Mary.

"Threatening ones. They tell me to leave town. Or ... or ..."

"When? How many letters have you had? Have you told the police?" Penny asked, aghast. She was excited about the new revelation but deeply concerned for the woman she now saw as vulnerable and alone. She drew Mary closer and gave her a hug, her earlier distaste for the gossiping woman forgotten.

Mary shook her head. "No, I haven't told anyone. I'm just a silly old biddy, aren't I? They won't take any notice, the police. Some people would say I'm getting what I deserve, no doubt."

"No, who would say that?"

"There are people in the town..." Mary tailed off.

Penny could understand that a lot of people would gossip and gloat, even if they stopped short of sending the letters themselves. "How many letters have you had?" Penny asked again.

"Four or five. The last one was three weeks ago. I'm so on edge waiting for the next one. I'm quite distracted."

Penny thought back. The last letter Mary had received was before David had been killed. Could he have been sending them to his own partner? It seemed very unlikely but of course, Penny had never met the man. In life, at any rate.

"Mary, do you have any idea who might have sent them?"

Mary's sobs were abating. She blew her nose again and

tucked the tissue away. "I always thought it was an ex-lover of his," she said. "I have a strong suspicion…"

She fell silent. Penny waited for her to finish but Mary began to pat her hair and pinch her cheeks, evidently readying herself to continue her walk. "You have a strong suspicion…" Penny prompted hopefully.

"It's gossip, nothing more." Mary threw her shoulders back and tipped her chin up, a woman determined to carry on in life and let nothing get her down. "Gossip's got me into so much trouble," she added, a downturn to her mouth.

"I … I was sorry to hear about the loss of your job," Penny said. "At the surgery."

Mary smiled tightly. "That? That was the least of it. Thank you, my duck, for your kindness today. Don't let me keep you from your walk. You be a good dog, now!" she said, wagging her finger at Kali. "Be good for your lovely owner!"

She patted Kali on the head and walked away, holding herself very straight and walking briskly. Penny watched her go, with Kali held close beside her on a tight lead. So, what other trouble had Mary's gossiping got her into?

And who had sent her the threatening letters?

CHAPTER FIFTEEN

"Hi Cath, or hi DC Pritchard if you're at work. It's Penny." Penny stood in her kitchen and stared out of the window, to where Kali was sniffing the hedge. She held the phone to her ear and leaned against the draining board.

"Ahh. Good morning. I'm at home. Has an officer been out to talk to you, yet?" Cath said.

"No, not yet. I was wondering if you were working later on today? You police have funny shifts."

"No. I've got a lazy Sunday planned. Hubby is taking the kids to one of those indoor play area things so they can jump around on multi-coloured balls or something. I think he secretly wants to have a go himself. No doubt I'll be receiving a call later informing me he's been banned or something."

"Brilliant. I've always fancied having a go myself.

Anyway, about that coffee you suggested yesterday..."

Cath laughed. "Okay, sure. Why don't you come over? I have the house to myself. If we go out to a coffee shop, I'll have to change out of my slobby clothes."

"You mean you won't be dressing for visitors?"

Cath snorted. "Nope. If you're lucky I'll brush my teeth. Come over any time after eleven."

"I'll bring cake."

"You'll run the gauntlet of Warren at the mini-market?" Cath asked. It was the only shop in Upper Glenfield open on a Sunday.

"Er … I'll make one," Penny declared impulsively.

"Smashing. I'm looking forward to it."

* * * *

It was some time after eleven that Penny made it to Cath's house. She stood on the doorstep clutching a plastic tub, feeling sheepish.

"Cake!" Cath declared as she swung open the door. She was wearing a faded grey pair of sweatpants and a loose long-sleeved top and looked every inch the weekend sofa-surfer.

"It's not exactly cake," Penny confessed. "It turned out I didn't have the basic ingredients. Like, er, eggs. I did have flour so instead I made biscuits. Sort of. I had to adapt the recipe. I used normal granulated sugar rather than fine caster sugar ... they might be a little, er, coarse."

"Are they packed with deliciously unhealthy calories?" Cath asked.

"Oh, definitely. I can guarantee calories."

"Perfect. Come on in!" Cath led her through to the garden room at the back of the house.

Penny prowled the long room while Cath made some hot drinks. The room had large windows that looked out over a grassy garden filled with children's toys. She hadn't seen it properly in the dark when she'd attended the kitchenware party. The garden room was warm and pleasant, with wicker furniture and potted plants and the occasional hard plastic building brick lying in wait underfoot. She took a seat on a comfortable wide chair, and opened the box of sort-of biscuits, sliding it onto a low round table.

"About last night–" Penny began when Cath had

returned and settled herself in a chair opposite.

"Hush!" Cath held up her hand. "It's okay. You really shouldn't be meddling. You will get into trouble. But … some of the stuff you've said did get me thinking and listening to gossip."

"You'll turn into Mary," Penny joked. "Incidentally, what exactly did she say to get sacked from the surgery?"

"Oh, it wasn't anything related to this. Just something to do with someone's terribly bad case of piles. The point was that it was a breach of trust. No one trusts her."

"I noticed," Penny said. "It was obvious at the craft group. So, what have you heard?"

"It's about Thomas and David's past."

Penny was excited. "Is it to do with the farm? Does it explain why the younger brother – David – inherited?"

"Everyone says that was because Thomas joined the Army and wasn't interested in the farm," Cath said. "I believe it. There's more, though. Here's the thing that I keep hearing on the sly. Their father, old Mr Hart, hated David and he was going to sell the farm because Thomas wouldn't take it on."

"No! Why would he hate his own son?"

Cath raised an eyebrow.

Penny sat forward, and asked, "And so how did David end up with the farm, then?"

"Well, apparently, old Mr Hart died first and he thought that verbal wishes were enough. They aren't. The farm automatically passed to his wife, on his death. And *she* made sure she had a water-tight will that did leave the farm to David."

"That makes sense," Penny said. "Just leave the farm to the son who wants it. But why did his father hate him? What had David done?"

"This is where the rumours get murkier," Cath said. "This one only started up last month, or at least, it's the first most people had heard of it. It's obvious when you think about it. David and Thomas's mother had had an affair. They were only half-brothers. David is someone else's son. And old Mr Hart knew it."

"Oh." Penny sat back again and sank into thought as she sipped her tea. It wasn't David's fault who his father was, or wasn't. It seemed monumentally unfair for Mr Hart to take against the innocent child like that.

But then, people were unfair, weren't they?

"How are the biscuits?" Penny asked.

Cath nibbled one. "Oaty. I think. And a bit …"

"Horrible?"

"Not exactly standard." Cath replaced it carefully on the table and smiled.

"The half-brother thing," Penny said, musing aloud. "You said it was a recent revelation? Who started it?"

"I don't know," Cath admitted.

"Could it have been Mary? She has form."

"Maybe. But how, and why? Why would she say something to upset her lover?"

Penny was nodding as it came together in her head. "She doesn't think before she speaks. She loves gossip for the sake of it. For the power of knowing something that other people didn't know. She and Eleanor were long-time friends, weren't they?"

"It seems unlikely but it's true."

"No, I don't see it's that unlikely, at all. Both are lonely women stuck here in a place they don't feel they quite belong in. Friendships get made over the strangest things. And then they had a falling-out over something unspecified. Perhaps Eleanor knew about Thomas and David's past.

That would make sense, because Eleanor is married to Thomas. Now if Eleanor told Mary in confidence, when she started dating David ... but Mary let it slip ..."

"Oh." Cath was nodding too.

"But the really big question is this," Penny said. "Did *David* know about his parentage and his past?"

"Everyone said he had been strange the past few weeks," Cath said. "That's why we had considered suicide at one point."

"That's it!" Penny cried. "I think we need to talk to Mary again!"

"Really?" Cath snorted a laugh. "You are already down on the records as harassing Eleanor and Thomas ... do you really want to make it three?"

CHAPTER SIXTEEN

Cath went off to make a fresh round of drinks. Penny sat back and tucked her heels up underneath her bottom, a position that used to be so natural to her. Pins and needles started up almost straight away and she knew she'd take a few minutes to unkink again when she tried to stand up.

Ugh. Ageing did not have many plus points.

She gazed around the garden room. One wall was devoted to framed photographs of the family. Many were artfully done in a photography studio, with everyone dressed in primary colours, posing against a stark white background. Wife, husband, two lively children.

She had to take a trip to see her parents soon, she thought. And what about her sister, Ariadne, and her hectic brood of children and her sullen, ignorant husband? Ariadne would defend him and his actions with her last breath but everyone could see how wrong she was. Penny didn't want a family like that.

Penny smiled and felt a strange pang of regret. Not for the childlessness – or childfree state, as she liked to consider it – but the lack of connection and unity that she had in her life. She refused to see it as empty. But there were corners that needed to be filled. Her career had been wonderful, fulfilling and amazing … but it didn't last. It was transient.

Then again, she mused as she looked at the happy portraits, family was also transient. Life ended. Consider poor David Hart, murdered for some unknown reason.

She was seized with a fresh burst of righteous enthusiasm. She had to make it right. The facts had to come out, for him and for her.

"More tea, vicar?" Cath joked as she came back through with a tray. "And I found some edible biscuits."

"Wonderful. Oh yes," she added as she munched one. "These are much better. I won't give up the day job, hey? I don't picture myself starting a bakery."

"Are you planning on working again?" Cath asked. "I know you came here to de-stress and all that, but aren't you going to get bored?"

"What's the upper age limit to join the police?" Penny asked, in half-seriousness.

Cath rolled her eyes at her. "Don't even think about it. There isn't an upper limit, as it happens. But…"

"Why not? Do you not recommend it as a fulfilling career?"

Cath glared at her.

Penny subsided. "It was just a thought. I have been doing a lot of art, as it happens. Mary got me thinking. I could design cards and do prints and all sorts."

"Go for it."

"Really? Just like that?"

"Yes," Cath said. "Other people do. So why not you? What is the difference between you, and someone who sells their art? The other person is trying. All you have to do, is do what they do."

"It sounds so easy."

"I'm sure it is. If you're prepared to work," Cath said. "Look at Drew. He's started doing those courses for rich folks who want to learn about, I don't know grass and stuff, and it's great."

"I met some people who sounded a bit negative about

it."

Cath shrugged. "A lot of people here don't like change and they don't like people trying new things."

"I got the feeling that was Drew himself."

"No, not at all. Drew is considered an alarmingly unpredictable go-getter around these parts."

"Wow." Penny considered that a frightening thought.

Cath laughed. "He's stubborn, but don't mistake that for stuck-in-the-mud. You could learn from him about starting up new businesses, to be honest."

Penny had to straighten her legs. She winced and wiggled her toes as the prickling started up in earnest. "If I do it, it does mean I am going to end up going to craft fairs with Mary."

"Consider it your penance for meddling in all this to start with."

"Huh." Penny stuck her tongue out childishly. "So did I tell you about the Taser?"

Cath stopped, her hand halfway to her mouth. An edge dropped from her biscuit into her tea. "What Taser? What on earth have you bought? They are not exactly legal, you know." Her eyes went to Penny's bag by her feet. "Please don't tell me…"

"Oh my goodness, no, I didn't. Buy one, I mean. Or tell you about it before. I should have told you last night. No, listen. I'm convinced now that the murderer is Thomas. That's what I was trying to tell you last night on the phone. When I went around to see Eleanor – I know, I know, I shouldn't have, I'm very sorry and all that, mea culpa – she threatened me with weapons. She said there was something in the house that would be able to stun me. Not a gun. There must be something like a Taser – do security guards use them?"

"Here in the UK? I don't think so. You need licences and reasons and all sorts for that sort of thing. Some police have them, but oh my goodness, the paperwork. Did she actually call it a Taser?"

"No. But look, there's more," Penny insisted. "I got a distinct impression that Eleanor is one of those aspirational sorts of women who like having manicures and read glossy magazines that features houses they can never afford. She seems totally unmatched with Thomas. He was shabby and unshaven and he is hardly a city high-flier. How much does night security guard pay?"

"Not a lot. It will be minimum wage stuff, I imagine. But they have been married a long time, and people do change. He was quite a catch in his youth, so I'm told."

"That's it," Penny said. "Thomas is jealous. He *was* jealous of the farm and the money it was making. The farm that he didn't want at first! And David has no wife and no kids. Did he leave a will? All his assets will go to Thomas if he hasn't left a will, won't it?"

"Oh yes…"

"Can you find out, Cath? Do you know if there was a will?"

"Leave it to me. I'll do some digging."

* * * *

A polite young man from the police station came to chat with Penny later that day. He found her in the back garden, trying to make sense of the mysterious plants and weeds that were emerging in the fertile soil.

"Is this supposed to be here?" she'd asked him, pointing at something dark green that emitted a sinister smell.

"I have no idea." He looked startled. "I'm from the police," he said, as if it wasn't obvious from his uniform. "It's about your antics last night..."

She plied him with tea and he accepted one of the awful biscuits. It was a credit to his courtesy that he manfully ate the whole thing with hardly a wince. She promised to be very good, and he advised her that any further reports of her harassment would be dealt with "severely and promptly."

And that was the end of that matter, except that she now had a "file" and the incident was logged in it.

The rest of Sunday was quiet. She pottered around, did some sketching, and spent some time trying to teach Kali to sit and stay. Kali could now stay in another room and patiently wait until she was called – at least, unless she was distracted by something, such as a passing car, a falling dust mote or an invisible current in the air.

She didn't hear from Cath again until Monday afternoon, by which time she was wild with frustration at not knowing what was going on. She was very close to just running out of the house and launching herself on Mary to ask her more questions. And she wondered if she ought to tell Cath about Mary's threatening letters. But it seemed like a betrayal of trust; it was up to Mary to decide what to do. She could hardly ride roughshod over another adult's personal decisions.

Still, she was uneasy about ignoring it, and she did pop to the shops to buy the right ingredients for a decent cake, with the intention of taking it around to Mary to show her support.

When Cath did call her, she sounded perky and excited. "I'm on my way home," she said, all faint and muffled. Penny guessed she was using her hands-free device in her car. "So I'm not technically working. First of all, was it PC Patel that came out to you yesterday?"

"Yes. He was a very pleasant and polite young man. He doesn't know anything about gardening, though.

"Er ... right. He called in sick today. You gave him a biscuit, didn't you?"

"Oh no. Sorry. Yes, I did. Is he okay?"

"I *hope* so. Anyway, the next thing is that Thomas was brought back in to the police station – okay, he was asked back, not arrested – to answer a few more questions. I shouldn't tell you this, and you never heard it from me, but his marriage was pretty rocky."

"I am utterly unsurprised."

"Well, yeah, but it's one thing to wonder about it, and another to have it confirmed from the horse's mouth. It was Eleanor. He says that she was having affairs."

"Not unusual," Penny said. "I can quite see that happening with her. I'm surprised that the local gossips didn't know, though." Bang goes your theory, Drew; not everyone knows everyone else's business.

"There's more!" Cath exclaimed. "Oh yes. Get this: before Thomas and Eleanor got married, she was actually going to marry David!"

"Oh." Penny stared at Kali, who was sitting at her feet. Kali blinked and looked away. "Oh wow…"

"Oh wow, indeed."

"Do you think they carried on seeing one another, even though she was now married to his brother? What happened? Why did she switch from one to the other?" Penny asked.

"I reckon that David simply wasn't glamorous enough. Remember, at that time, Thomas was jetting around the world while David was working the farm. As for whether they continued to see one another once she was married …

I don't know."

"This just gives you even more motives and reasons to suspect Thomas," Penny said. "And you guys released him?"

"It's nothing to do with me. I'm sorry. Look … I'm home now. Don't let on that I told you any of this, all right?"

"You're secretly enjoying the chase as much as I am, aren't you?" Penny said.

"No. Maybe. Yes, of course, because it's my job."

"Yes… and I'm helping, aren't I?"

"No."

"Yes."

"I need to go in and get the oven on."

"You're loving this."

"Go away. I'm getting out of the car. I'm finishing this call."

"La la la I'm not listening," Penny said with a laugh.

"Bye."

When the call ended, Penny remained sitting on her sofa, her sketchbook loose in her hands. She was happy. She felt like she had a new friend. And she was deeply frustrated that it was so blindingly obvious that Thomas

Hart had killed his brother, and no one seemed to be doing anything about it.

CHAPTER SEVENTEEN

On Tuesday morning Penny was in the kitchen, sliding Mary's cake into the oven, when Kali went nuts in the hallway. It was the regular post delivery, which never failed to ignite foaming fury in the dog. How dare the postman come onto *her* property? No matter that Penny had patiently introduced the dog to the postman on frequent occasions, and that if they met outside, she would bound up to him expecting a treat.

"You daft dog," Penny grumbled as she wiped her hands on a towel and wandered down the hallway to rescue the slightly-chewed letters from the mat. There was one junk mail circular, and one letter, with a Lincoln postmark and the address printed in unsteady capital letters.

It looked very odd. She patted Kali absently and walked back to the kitchen. She set the timer for the cake, and then stood by the window as she opened the curious envelope.

There was one sheet of A4 paper inside, folded four times. She flattened it out and her stomach felt cold.

The message was written in thick black marker pen, in the same shaky capitals as the address.

It was a stark, blunt warning.

GET OUT

Penny's hands shook. It was irrational, but she folded it up and then unfolded it again, as if it would become a different message. But it was no magic trick.

It was a threat.

Mary's letters had told her to go away, too. Now it was imperative that Penny spoke with Mary again. She had to compare the letters to determine if they came from the same source. That would rule out David as the sender of them – unless there was something supernatural going on, which she highly doubted.

But then, this was Lincolnshire, after all.

* * * *

It was difficult to wait for the cake to cook. Finally she

pulled it out of the oven and left it to cool. While it rested on the wire rack, she decided to go out and visit Drew in his forge. She needed to be active and doing something to distract herself from the letter.

She had to let Cath and the police know. She was sure of that. But she was also determined to find out a little more and see if it was linked to Mary's letters. She wasn't sure if she was going to tell Drew or not, but she wanted to.

But he had told her he didn't want to be any part of it. He knew she was going to talk to Eleanor and he had disagreed and walked away.

Penny walked more and more slowly as she neared the industrial area. There was an agricultural vehicle showroom, with glossy, shiny tractors in a row outside. There was some kind of small-scale catering operation, and two white-coated workers leaned out of a fire exit to smoke some cigarettes, their blue hairnets pushed back on their heads.

And there was the forge. She stopped in the shared car parking area and looked across the tarmac to the open doors. So, he was in there. She could hear the repetitive tap-tap-bang, tap-tap-bang as something magical happened to metal as it became a useful or ornamental item.

He'd walked away from her.

He'd shown her kindness. She owed him for the head-collar and the support he had shown.

She was torn.

Men made things complicated, she thought, somewhat crossly. No wonder I avoided any of my relationships becoming serious. Although in truth, I was always too busy to notice if they were getting serious or not, and eventually the men gave up and wandered off, calling me "commitment shy" as they left.

The tapping had stopped. A figure crossed the open space of the doors, pausing halfway.

Her stomach lurched and she turned abruptly, and walked quickly away from the scene. Men were too complicated, she told herself again.

Finally she decided to call Francine back, and she fished her mobile phone from her bag as she went briskly along the High Street and back to her cottage.

* * * *

The conversation with Francine was short as she was

about to go into a meeting.

"You have already forgotten what it's like to work for a living," Francine said with a laugh. "It's Tuesday. Normal people are working."

"Oh my goodness. Yes, I did forget."

"Quick, tell me about the craft group."

Penny slowed her pace. "I haven't spoken to you since that? Oh no. There was Mary and then Ginni but she was angry and then Eleanor and Thomas but I don't have an ASBO but someone has sent me a threat, so…"

"What are the police doing about it?"

"I haven't told them," Penny confessed.

Penny didn't need the miracle of telephone technology to hear Francine's shriek. "Go to the police right now!" There was a muffled conversation then, as Francine told someone she was *on her way, hold on, wait*. "Sorry. Just asking them to hang on with the meeting. I really have to go. But Penny, please, go to the police. I'll call you as soon as I can. How exciting!"

And that was that.

How exciting?

Penny shook her head at Francine's exuberance.

Everything had changed now. It wasn't an exciting bit of fun. Someone had threatened her – her, Penny – and she felt sick, vulnerable. And alone.

She let herself into her cottage, and buried her face in Kali's fur for a moment, sunk to her knees in the hallway. "Hey, there, girl. We'll be all right."

Kali's tail thumped the floor. Penny had to take that as a yes. The smell of baking was filling her nostrils, and it was time to attend to the cake.

She threw herself into the mechanics of cooking and decorating. She whipped up some buttercream filling and sandwiched the Victoria sponge cake together, adding a layer of jam as well. She dusted some icing sugar over the top, and sat down to admire it. Kali came and pressed against her leg, hopeful that some of the lovely-smelling cake would somehow just mysteriously fall to the floor for her to helpfully eat.

The letter was sitting on the table, its message stark and unequivocal. GET OUT.

She felt a heavy, dragging unwillingness to go and see Mary. Her imagination was now working overtime. Was it a bluff by Mary to garner sympathy? Was it someone dangerous? Was it the murderer?

What would happen if she did not GET OUT?

There was no threat spelled out. Was that going to come in the next letter?

She laid her head on her arms briefly and closed her eyes. Maybe Drew was right and she should never have meddled.

* * * *

When she awoke, her mouth was dry and her head was fuzzy. Her shoulders ached and popped as she straightened up. What a stupid position to fall asleep in, she thought.

The cake.

The cake was gone.

Her first thought linked it to the threatening letter, until she saw the sheepish look on Kali's face – not to mention the icing sugar around her muzzle. Half of it was in pieces on the floor. Penny leaped to her feet with a cry and Kali dashed away looking guilty.

"Oh no. What am I going to take to Mary now?" It felt like the last straw. Penny hadn't realised how much it was all getting to her until this moment. On her knees, scraping up the destroyed cake, with a scary letter on the table; she wanted to curl up and cry.

Like in London, when she had begun to realise that stress was making her ill.

No. She sat back on her heels and took a deep breath. She was in control, she told herself. Kali peeped around the door and Penny remembered what she had read about the guilty look in dogs; it was really fear, not guilt. She called Kali over and rubbed her head. Kali rolled onto her back, which unfortunately smeared the jam a little more over the kitchen floor. The dog was going to need a bath.

"Oh, you." Penny started to giggle, and then to laugh. She had to see the funny side. "Get up, daft dog."

Kali sprang to her feet and looked at her feet in confusion. Penny cleared up and wiped the floor. She grabbed some antibacterial wipes designed for pets and made a valiant attempt to clean the remnants of the cake out of Kali's fur, much to the dog's disgust. "I'm sorry. Were you saving that for later? Look after the house, and try not to be sick," she told the dog. "I have a mission." She picked up the letter and went to see Mary.

* * * *

Penny expected Mary's house to be in some sort of hippy-clutter-disarray with dream catchers and multi-coloured wall hangings and the lingering scent of patchouli.

She was very wrong.

Mary opened the front door of her terraced cottage cautiously, peering through a four-inch gap until she recognised Penny, and then she flung the door open with a cry of greeting. "Now then! Penny, my duck!"

"Hello, Mary. How are you?"

"Fair to middling. Not so dusty. Come in, come in."

Penny stepped into a pristine living room, the front door opening directly from the street. It was a large, low-ceilinged, square room, with plain magnolia-yellow walls and a beige three-piece suite with dark red cushions. There were no bookshelves, a fact which always made Penny shudder in other people's houses.

"Would you like a drink?" Mary asked. She looked like she was standing in the wrong house, dressed in her layers of velvet with her jangling bangles and fringed shawl.

"No, thank you. I'm afraid I'm here with some difficult questions. Um." Penny fiddled with her bag and pulled out the envelope. She decided it was in no one's interest to mess around. "I received this letter this morning and I wondered if it was similar to the ones you had got."

Mary's face tensed and she took half a step backwards, her hands raised in front of her, and her fingers flexing at nothing. She stared at the letter in Penny's hand. "Can I see?" she whispered.

Penny unfolded it and began to pass it over, but Mary could see the words printed there and she waved it away. "Oh, oh," she said. "Yes. Wait. I'll get mine."

Penny would have found Mary's reaction comical if she hadn't, herself, received a letter. When it actually happened to you, she reflected, it was a whole new thing, and quite sickening.

Mary went through the door at the far end of the room, and returned a moment later with two sheets of paper. "These are the last few I got," she said, and thrust them at Penny with a trembling hand.

LEAVE TOWN NOW said one, and GET OUT OR ELSE said the other, with an added unpleasant profane insult scrawled at the bottom of the sheet. It was the same handwriting, the same paper, and the same style of envelope.

"Was yours addressed to you?" Mary asked.

"Yes. To Miss Penny May. I am actually a Ms.," she added. "And yours?"

"Miss Mary Radcliffe. I *am* a Miss."

"We need to tell the police," Penny said.

"No, no, no," Mary moaned. "I can't. I'm sorry, Penny, I just can't, duck. I've never spoken to them. Never."

"The police are there to help us," Penny said, as if lecturing a small child.

Mary began to pace around her room, crossing to the mantelpiece over the gas fire and moving one of the delicate china ornaments a micro-millimetre to the left, and then back to the right. "No, no. They will ask questions and I'll get flustered and it's all my own fault. It's all my fault. Me, you see. Just a silly old woman who can't keep her mouth shut. But I'm learning, see, my duck, I'm learning." She turned and faced Penny with a set, hard face. "So I shan't talk to the police."

Silence fell between them. Penny didn't feel right in

trying to put pressure on an already fragile woman.

There was nothing for Penny to do but to leave, and return home, thoughtful.

Mary had said it was all her fault: what else had she to be sorry for?

CHAPTER EIGHTEEN

Penny found herself moping around for two days. Francine did call back, and Penny filled her in, but made light of it all, and Francine's reaction was one of shared excitement. Penny realised that to Francine, she was simply watching a thrilling film, divorced from the reality that Penny was actually living through.

In truth, the letter had deeply unsettled her but she decided not to tell anyone in Upper Glenfield about it. Instead, she waited to see if she would receive another, but the post on Wednesday and Thursday brought her nothing but junk mail and a bank statement.

The bank statement wasn't sobering, exactly, but it reminded her that she had to think more about her future here in Upper Glenfield. She could tighten her belt a little, and manage perfectly well, but life would be small and constrained. Penny had never wanted to live a small, constrained life. She had earned the right to splash out on nice food now and then, she thought. Her plans to go to craft fairs resurfaced.

So she spent some long hours curled on her sofa with her sketchbook, and even more hours out with Kali and her cheap digital camera, snapping reference shots to play about with on the computer later on. She was not getting used to the lack of internet and she dreaded to imagine how many emails she'd find when the engineer finally came out to put the necessary boxes in place for a phone line.

Through all her wandering and moping and sketching, she didn't pursue the murder case any longer in her thoughts, in spite of Francine's urging. She was fed up of it. The letter bothered her but she was afraid to think it might be linked – though it had to be. She had annoyed Eleanor and Thomas; she could quite imagine that the letter came from them. Why would one of them have sent threats to Mary, though? Mary was still hiding something, and she was still a suspect, in Penny's mind.

But it was not her case, Penny told herself sternly. Restrain yourself, woman. Know your place and all that.

Listen to Drew, not Francine.

She started to avoid phone calls from Francine again.

* * * *

It was mid-afternoon on Thursday when it all changed. Penny was sitting at her kitchen table with her sketchbook, armed with some glue and a pair of scissors, feeling like she was back at art school again as she chopped and rearranged some drawings of foliage that she had made. The shapes were suggesting some repeating pattern that would look good stencilled onto plain linen and perhaps turned into a simple tote bag.

Kali knew someone was at the door before the knock, as usual, but her bark was a happy, short one rather than the "get off my property you vile postman" tirade. Penny expected to see Cath, or even Mary, but she was surprised.

It was Drew, holding a small posy of flowers and looking very contrite.

"Hi, I'm an idiot," he said, shuffling his feet.

"Hi, yes you are. Come on in." Penny's first feeling was one of pleasure and warmth, but tinged then with surprise and suspicion. If he was going to tell her what to do, he could leave right now. But she decided to hear what he had to say. It was always nice when people brought you flowers, after all.

He trailed after her to the kitchen and stopped when he saw her artistic efforts, the sheets of paper spread out on the table. "I like that," he said, pointing to the uppermost sketch. "It's goosegrass. I think it's a very underrated plant."

"Goosegrass?"

"This one," he said, pointing at the sketch of the leggy, trailing weed with its sticky round balls. "You can eat it, but it's not great raw."

"I can't imagine it's a culinary delight even when it's cooked. We called it cleavers as kids. Because it, er, cleaves, I suppose. We used to stick it to each other's backs."

"Well, there's no cleavers or goosegrass in this," he said, thrusting the posy forward. "It's garden grown. I don't go picking wild flowers."

"I'm glad to hear it. How lovely! Thank you. I'll get a jam jar. I didn't bother bringing any vases when I moved."

He looked awkward and out of place, standing in her kitchen. He was too big for houses – not physically, but just the way he seemed to want to leap out of doors and escape. She had a flash of inspiration. "Shall we go for a walk? I want to show you how good Kali's being with the head-collar."

"Yes. I'd like that."

And so they found themselves rambling west out of town, along the river, under the bridge and out into the hillier land. The weather was warm but the sky was grey and overcast, with a muggy tint to the air. To Penny's delight, Kali did, indeed, behave impeccably.

"It's good the way she checks in with you as she walks," Drew observed. "See how she is always looking back to see where you are. You should reward her with a treat now and then, for that. You're bonding."

Penny felt a warmth surge from her belly. A bond? After everything, and all her doubts especially in the first few days, it was lovely to think that she had done the right thing after all. "Thank you. That means a lot to me." Of course that jinxed it. "Oh – Kali, no. No! The nettles! Leave it. Come here!" She enticed the dog out of the tempting patch of stinging weeds and they continued along the dry path.

"You know stuff," she said to Drew. "So tell me. What's the point of nettles? They're just horrible."

"They are tasty in spring," he said. "In the hungry gap, they're really useful as a source of iron."

"Ouch. Tingly, too! I think I'd rather have a go at eating cleavers."

"They don't sting when you eat them. They make a good soup."

"So what's the hungry gap?" she asked.

"We're coming out of it now. At the end of winter, and into spring, the food stores are running low, traditionally. But new growth isn't coming through much yet. So although the countryside gets all lush and verdant, actually, there's a very real danger of starvation. Historically speaking."

"Oh, right."

He bent and grabbed a nettle by the root, making Penny wince as he squeezed tightly and wrenched it free from the soil. "And the fibres inside can be spun or made into ropes," he continued. "You know that folk tale about the woman who had to spin fine shirts for the swans to turn them back into men again, but she had to use nettles? It's possible." He pulled a pocket knife out and split the long stem, revealing the white stringy mass within.

Penny was fascinated. "Wow. Real nettle shirts. Okay. So nettles might have a purpose."

"They tell us about the landscape, too." Drew was alight with enthusiasm now. "They need a lot of phosphate in the ground to grow and get all nice and deep green. That's likely along the edges of fields that have had fertilisers added, but also wherever humans have lived in the past too. It's a clue to the history of a place."

"How do you know all this stuff?" Penny could see why he was running courses now.

He shrugged and cast the nettle stem back into the patch. "I've picked it up over the years. I talk to old folks, I like poking around in old bookshops, and I spend a lot of time out and about, observing stuff."

"I bet your courses are amazing," she said.

He laughed. "They are fun."

They were silent for a little while, then as they reached the top of a ridge, he spoke again.

"There's one big thing we haven't talked about."

Her heart thudded twice and her mouth went dry.

"This murder case," he went on, before she could speak and make an utter fool of herself.

"Oh – oh yes. I've left it alone. Honestly."

"Really?" He didn't sound convinced but when she stole a sideways glance at him, he was smiling very slightly.

"Mm."

"What happened?" he asked her. "They haven't found the killer, have they? It would have been hot news if they had. Even I would have heard about it."

"No, they've not been found. It's just…"

They stood side by side, looking out over a Lincolnshire panorama of rolling hills that fell away to the flat Fenlands in the far distance, the atmosphere blurring the green fields into blue. Upper Glenfield nestled below them, a pretty town with the western bypass curling like a grey snake between the houses and the spot where they stood up on the ridge. It was easier to talk to someone when you didn't face them directly, Penny thought. That was how so many of her love affairs and relationships had ended; the painful conversations had taken place in cars, for some reason, with both parties staring dead ahead through the glass.

She plunged into a summary of events. "So, I went to talk to Eleanor and she threatened me and then I went to see Thomas but he chased me away and then they told the police, obviously, so an officer came around to tell me off but I sort of accidentally poisoned him with a biscuit and then I got a letter telling me to get out of town and that's it, really."

There was an extended silence.

"Start again," said Drew eventually. "But with more gaps. And, you know, some actual explanation."

* * * *

Drew, like Francine, tried to convince her that she had to tell the police about the letter. He spent the whole return journey persuading her that it was not only in her own interests, but also that of Mary's, and anyone else who had had received such threats. Eventually, she was convinced, and agreed to speak to Cath as soon as she could.

When they were at the bottom of River Street, Penny invited him to her cottage for a coffee, but he refused.

"I've got some thinking and planning to do," he said.

"I can't keep on running two businesses. I need to make a choice between the smithing, and the field-craft. Everyone I've spoken to has told me to stay with a solid craft and ignore the flighty field-craft courses. But…"

"Ahh. You need to follow what makes you happy, as much as the money."

"I know. But it's hard. Anyway, with running my own businesses, it's about control as much as it's about money, for me."

"That's why a lot of people go self-employed."

"Yeah. So anyway. I think I'm going to go against the gossips and well-meaning meddlers of Glenfield and do my own thing. And as for you … speak to Cath!" he added as she turned to go.

"I will!"

* * * *

But as soon as she got home, she unclipped Kali from the head-collar and stood in the kitchen, frozen in thought, halfway through the act of putting the kettle on.

Drew's words stuck in her head.

Not the nettles thing, though that was interesting, or even the new plans that he had for his future.

"It's about control as much as it's about money."

Control. Not money.

Control. Not money.

If it was all about money, then Mary or Thomas would have killed David. That was clear.

But if it was about *control* …

Eleanor and David had dated. They had been supposed to marry. But Eleanor had pursued glamour – she wanted a rich, attractive, powerful man – and she'd turned to his more appealing brother. Meanwhile, David had remained single, but with various lovers, over the years.

And Eleanor had had lovers too, once the shine of being married to Thomas had worn off, and his career had nose-dived, and he was no longer the James Bond-type she had married.

Perhaps Eleanor and David *had* got back together.

Something had happened. Because at the time of his death, he had been seeing Mary, not Eleanor.

Mary was Eleanor's friend. No, she was her ex-friend. They'd been close friends for a long time until recently…

Penny's heart was hammering double-time as it fell into place, each thought slotting into its hole with a satisfying click.

Thomas might have had a Taser and this meant *Eleanor had access to it.*

Thomas had the means but Eleanor was the one with the motivation. Perhaps she only meant to punish him, not to kill him! Penny slammed the kettle back onto the stand and dashed through the cottage to find her mobile phone. She had to speak to Cath – urgently.

There were unanswered questions and the edge of danger about it all. She'd been threatened and so had Mary – Penny now decided that those threats had to have come from Eleanor, and if she'd killed once out of malice and control, who knew what she would do next?

Cath's number just rang right through to voicemail. Infuriated, Penny left a message.

"Cath! It's Penny. It was Eleanor! She killed David. I've got a letter. Not a confession, I mean, a threat, it kind of links it all together, aargh. I really need to talk to you. Call me. Right now. I'm coming up to Lincoln, I'll find you.

No, don't call when I'm driving, I don't have hands-free, but–"

The voicemail storage ran out of space and the phone beeped at her. Penny flung it into a bag and grabbed her car keys from the bowl by the front door.

"Guard the house," she told the bemused Kali. "I'll be back later."

She drove like a loon to Cath's house but as she suspected, it was empty and quiet.

Next stop, Lincoln police station.

CHAPTER NINETEEN

It was rush hour in the city of Lincoln and she still hadn't worked out the easiest routes around the place. The city seemed to have two centres – there was the old part of town, the Bailgate area, which was at the top of the imaginatively-named Steep Hill with the castle and the cathedral and its twisty cobbled streets of souvenir shops. But at the bottom of the hill (or, indeed, The Hill) was a more modern maze of shopping areas, with some roads being traffic-free and some with an inexplicable one-way system around them. It was bisected by a pleasant river, and more annoyingly, a main railway line. At peak times, the crossing barriers seemed to be down, blocking the traffic, for far longer periods than they were raised. Busy times in Lincoln seemed to consist of everyone staying exactly where they were, but getting angrier by the minute.

She followed some contradictory signs for a car park. They must be puzzle signs, she through in exasperation as she was directed down a side street and then abandoned, with no further signage or hints as to which way she should turn. She should have come on the bike, she thought ruefully. Though the old thumper was a lot slower than her car, what she lost in travel time, she'd make up for in ease of parking. Eventually she was able to leave the car in an on-street parking bay. She expected that she wasn't going to have the right change for the ticket machine but the goblins of mischief relented and the meter accepted her slew of silverware. Soon she was on her way to the police station on foot.

There was a plethora of entrances but she ran up the steps to the public reception. There was an open waiting area, doors with buzzers and keypad entries, and one man behind a sheet of plastic under a sign marked "Enquiries." He was writing in a notebook but he looked up as Penny hurled herself into the reception area.

"I'm looking for Cath! Detective Constable Pritchard!" she said breathlessly.

He seemed to take forever to lay down his pen and

reply. "Now then. Is she expecting you?"

"Yes. No. No! I left her a message. On her phone. She hasn't replied. It's urgent."

"And may I ask what it is concerning…?"

"A murder!"

He raised one eyebrow but his whole demeanour remained placid and unruffled. Even his tone of voice didn't change. "Is anyone's life in immediate danger? Have you dialled 999? I think there are many officers here who are capable of dealing with such incidents. Not just DC Pritchard. We're all trained, you know. Even in Lincolnshire."

She ignored the jibe at her southern accent which marked her out as an incomer. "No, he's already dead. I mean, it was a while ago. The murder. I've worked out who it was!"

"The deceased? Do *we* know about it?"

"Yes, of course you do. Please, is Cath here? Can you, I don't know, radio to her or something?"

The man laughed and shook his head. "Can I take your name, please, madam?"

"Look, I–"

One of the internal doors clicked and sprang open, and a very tall, very wide female officer came through, speaking to the man behind her. "That's quite understandable, Mr Hart. Thank you for your time."

"Thomas! Oh my goodness, have you been arrested? Let him go," Penny shouted to the bewildered officer. "He's not the murderer!"

"That I'm not!" Thomas said. "Hey, I recognise you. It's the pest from the other night! Officer, this woman is harassing both me, and my wife. I've already spoken to the police about *you*. Haven't they put a restraining order on you or something?"

"Is that why you're here?" Penny asked, smiling nervously at the frowning officers. This could get messy.

"No." He glowered at her. "They asked me to come and talk about my wife, that's all. Not that it is any of your business." He shook his head, and looked suddenly sad. "There's a murderer out there and all they can do is bother innocent people. My brother, murdered. I know we hadn't got on, but he was still my brother. And he didn't deserve what happened to him. None of it. All his life."

"Where is Eleanor?" Penny said desperately.

He shrugged. "It's none of your business," he repeated.

She pulled out the piece of paper with the threat scrawled on it. "Well, she sent me this! Now who is harassing who?"

"You said you were here about a murder," the desk sergeant said from behind the plastic screen. "Not harassment."

"I am. I'm here about both, I suppose. Please. I know I haven't made a great first impression but it's about the murder of David Hart. Thomas is innocent…"

"I know," Thomas said angrily. "I just told you that."

"But his wife is not!" Penny blurted out, loudly.

"How dare you!"

"Listen. Please." She waved the paper in the air. "I'm sorry, Thomas. I suppose you knew that before you married Eleanor, she was involved with your brother David? And that she … oh goodness, this is horrible, I am so sorry. But while you've been married…" She couldn't say it.

But he could. He went puce in the face and muttered, "Yes, yes. I know. She had affairs. I am not good enough for her."

"Oh, Thomas." Penny did feel pain for the man. But

she continued. "So, well, so she did have these affairs. And maybe one was with David. But when Mary started seeing David, Eleanor was jealous. She couldn't stand it. I know you've got some device like a Taser or something, Thomas. Eleanor had access to it. Maybe she didn't mean to kill him, but ... but now he is dead."

"Have you any evidence for these serious accusations?" the tall female officer asked.

"I've got the threats she sent me – and Mary."

"Mary?" Thomas said. "What threats?"

"I know Mary hasn't reported it, but she has had some of these letters too. Mary Radcliffe," she added for the benefit of the officers. "It's all about the farm, and jealousy, but not from Thomas. Eleanor was jealous of the money David had. The fact that the farm should never have gone to him, according to..."

Thomas hung his head. "According to my father."

"Did you know about David's parentage?" Penny asked.

"I never knew who his real father was, no. But from an early age it was obvious that something was different about David. At first I followed my father's lead. He would bully him something terrible. Then I just wanted to get away. Maybe that was spineless of me, I don't know, but it was like I was being asked to choose between my parents and I couldn't, so I left. I was glad when he got the farm, I really was! David was a good farmer."

"I believe you," Penny said. "Did David know his real father?"

"Until recently, he didn't even know our dad … my dad … wasn't his real father."

Penny was shocked. "You knew, but he didn't? How did he find out?"

"He heard it through gossip and rumours."

"Who gossiped?" Penny asked, fearing she knew the answer. More things were falling into place. She felt desperately sad for both David and Thomas, two half-brothers who had argued yet who were linked together more than they realised.

"Mary, of course," Thomas confirmed. "She found out, and she talked. And David heard about it … what a way to find out. He never ought to have found out. It shouldn't have mattered. It's why I never said anything. What would be the point?"

And that was why Mary was feeling so guilty. When

David had been found dead, and they'd thought it was suicide at first, she must have been distraught, and blamed herself, Penny thought. What a mess. "And Mary knew because Eleanor told her?" Penny asked.

"Yes, I suppose so."

Penny looked imploringly at the officer standing beside Thomas. "You must find Eleanor!" she told her. "She is the killer. Don't you see, Thomas? I'm so sorry."

The female officer twisted her mouth and frowned. "Hmm. Let's back up a moment. This Taser or whatever …"

Thomas's shoulders sagged even further. "Yes. I did have one. I do. I did. The thing is, it went missing, and of course I didn't report it because I should never have had it in the first place."

The officer behind the screen stood up. The female officer next to Thomas appeared to get even taller.

"You had a Taser and it went missing…" she repeated. "Right. I suggest you tell me where we might find your wife, sir. And don't even *think* about telling me it's none of *my* business…"

The police station seemed to erupt into action around

them, but Penny was a still and silent centre as the officers whirled around. She was asked to step to one side, and then ushered into a bare waiting room, and after half an hour was offered a pale cup of tea.

She paced and she prowled as she waited for news, until finally Cath appeared in the doorway, smiling.

"We've got her."

CHAPTER TWENTY

"I think summer is finally here!" Mary announced as she entered the community hall looking as unsummery as it was possible to be, in her long black skirt and fringed purple cardigan.

Everyone else at the craft group was wearing pale pastels and fanning themselves with pieces of paper, including Penny. She greeted Mary with a wave and a nod, and the older woman immediately ambled over and took a seat next to Penny.

The others didn't sidle away, exactly, but Mary couldn't attract close friends, even after the truth came out about the murder, and how she'd been an unwilling victim of the hate mail sent by Eleanor. People were sympathetic to her plight, but no one could forget how harmful her particular type of gossip was.

But Penny had time for her. She felt a strange bond of obligation to Mary; they'd both received those letters and they shared the fright and pain of it. They had attended some craft fairs together, and Penny had been surprised at how much fun she had. The fun factor was increased by the fact she actually earned some money, of course.

Although it was somewhat awkward when Mary's sales still consistently didn't even cover the cost of her table hire.

Ginni came up behind them as Mary unloaded her cards and papers onto the table. "Mary, Penny. Oh, Penny! What a lovely drawing."

Penny was finishing a sketch of Kali. She'd used a range of dark, soft pencils and a looser style than she usually employed. She was quite pleased with it, and thought that it might make a nice set of prints for coasters and table mats and the like. "Thank you."

"How is she doing?" Ginni asked. "Your dog, I mean. I saw you walking with her when you first moved in but didn't manage to say hello ... you were being dragged at some speed along the road, I'm afraid."

"I'm pleased to say that hardly ever happens now. Unless I walk her close to her feeding time and she decides she wants to get home."

Ginni laughed. "I'm glad to hear it. Well done."

* * * *

Drew must have been lying in wait for her as she left the hall to walk home. He was leaning against a wall, and pushed forward as soon as he spotted her. He was wearing his standard set of faded jeans, but as a nod to the warm sunshine, he was sporting a white tee-shirt rather than his lumberjack shirt or enormous and ragged-elbowed jumper.

"Now then," he said in greeting.

"Now then," she replied, grinning. How Lincolnshire was she? "How is the business going?" she asked, as he fell into step alongside her.

He laughed. "Depends on who you listen to. I was in the mini-market last week, and I overheard Agatha telling everyone within earshot that it was such a shame my blacksmithing business has failed. They were all clicking their tongues and saying I seemed like such a nice young man, how tragic."

"But it hasn't failed. You've changed direction, that's

all. Did you set them right?"

"No, there's no point. I'm doing something dangerously different and I am something to be feared."

She rolled her eyes on his behalf.

He nodded. "Yup. It's easier for you because you're an incomer so everyone expects you to be a little unreliable and odd. You can get away with anything, really. Me, I'm bound by history and heritage and all that malarky."

"I never thought of it that way. Does your family all live in Upper Glenfield?" she asked.

"Yes, and all my uncles and aunts and cousins are here or in the nearby villages, except for Uncle Jim who moved to Bristol and set up a micro-brewery with a man called Lawrence who wears the most extraordinary dresses. I was the only one from here who went to their wedding."

"Oh."

"And my brother Ross, he lives in Lincoln and does something terribly sciencey. Mum and dad live south of here, on a smallholding. And yourself? You've never mentioned your own family."

Penny's pace slowed. "My mum and dad are currently on the Orient Express somewhere. They are getting old quite disgracefully and I think it's wonderful. I get random postcards from them, from time to time. I have a sister, Ariadne, but we don't get on."

"That sounds quite final."

"Well, we don't. She has issues but she won't accept help so that's that."

Drew opened his mouth and then closed it again, and she was grateful that he didn't pursue the matter. They continued on for a few yards. Penny tipped her head back to let the sun warm her skin.

"Uh-oh. Up ahead, just past the phone box," Drew said, startling Penny out of her sun-worship.

She strained her eyes, expecting to see a rare bird or something. But it was Warren, just coming around the corner, carrying his camera with the long, intimidating zoom lens. When he saw them together, he stopped, and openly stared, his fleshy face unfriendly and flat. Penny and Drew walked past. She couldn't resist greeting him cheerily, but Warren did not respond.

"What is his issue?" she asked when they were out of earshot. "It's like he thinks every woman in the world should be grateful for his attention and he gets annoyed when they are not."

"That's exactly his issue," Drew said. "I don't think it's any more complicated than that."

"Sad, really. What relationships and love make people do."

"You're thinking about David Hart again, aren't you?"

"I am." Penny kicked at the ground with her sandals as they passed the market area and came to the crossroads in the centre of town. "It seems such a waste of a life. Not just David's. I mean Eleanor's."

When the police had gone to the house, they had found Eleanor sitting on her sofa, staring blankly into space. It was as if she knew what was coming, Cath had told Penny afterwards. Eleanor had broken down and confessed to being driven by jealousy and spite – and anger at David, not at Mary.

David had been seeing Eleanor, behind her husband's back, off and on for many years. Eventually he had grown tired of her and finished with her for good. But when he'd taken up with Mary, she'd seen it as a deliberate blow against herself. She'd known his habits and his routines. Finding him out alone in the fields was easy.

Had she meant to kill him? She said that she hadn't. She'd been told that a Taser couldn't kill.

But it could, and it did.

And now she was in a women's prison. Penny didn't know of anyone who had been to visit her. Thomas had moved away immediately; the rumours said he was in a bedsit in Lincoln. Their marital home was still up for sale, the grass outside now unkempt and long, the pristine lawn ruined through lack of care.

"People do get stuck in a way of thinking," Drew said, "and the longer they go on, the harder it is for them to change, I suppose."

They stood still and silent for a moment.

Drew shook himself. "Anyway. Let's go on a picnic."

"When?"

"Tomorrow. Bring Kali."

"Will you teach me about plants and things?"

"Of course. I'll show you which ones you can eat."

"Oh," she said with a laugh. "So I don't need to bring a picnic, then? We can just eat our way around the hedgerows of Upper Glenfield."

"Sure. Just bring some salad cream. That's the one

thing that doesn't grow locally."

There was an awkward moment when Penny wondered if Drew was going to hug her or something more, but their eyes met and he laughed, and stepped backwards. Her stomach fluttered and she chided herself for wanting something while at the same time, not wanting it at all.

Things were fine as they were.

"I'll see you tomorrow," she said hastily, starting down the street to her cottage.

"I'll call at ten."

"Great."

She didn't look back but she felt strangely warm in the pit of her belly as she strode down the pavement. She was almost humming to herself as she flung the cottage door open.

"Hello, Kali! What have you been up to, hey?" she said, bending to scratch the happy dog behind the ears.

"Oh. That's what you've been up to."

Her new strappy sandals, an impulse purchase from a boutique shop in Lincoln, lay in shreds across the hallway carpet.

She stood up straight and glared at the dog for a

moment.

"Oh well. Walking boots will be a better choice tomorrow, anyway. Come on. Shall we go walkies?"

They went.

The End...

...for now.

Coming soon: Small Town Secrets! Sign up to my mailing list for news of each release here: http://issybrooke.com/newsletter/

I don't send emails at any other time, so you won't drown in spam about this and that.

Did you know - leaving a review can make a huge difference to an independent author? We're not looking for a million 5-star reviews. It's far more helpful to have a considered and critical few sentences outlining what worked, what did not work, and who might enjoy the book. So please spare a few minutes to add your feedback to this book's page on Amazon. Thank you!

Author's Afterword

This is the bit you don't need to read, but if you enjoyed the book you might want to find out more.

I've got a website at http://www.issybrooke.com where I have more information about the characters, about Lincolnshire, and the fictional town of Glenfield - including a map.

The dog in this story, Kali, is based on our own rescue dog, a Rottie cross called Stella. That's her on the cover of this book. She's a stressed out and reactive thing, and we're still working through her issues. I wish it was as easy as Penny found it … you can read more about dogs on my website, too. And look at photos. Everyone loves photos of dogs, right?

There are more books coming in this series (I wrote a heap all at once). So you can check out what Penny gets up to next in Small Town Secrets. Does she get any further with Drew? Will Francine re-appear? Is Cath a new friend? Is Warren a new enemy?

Oh, I'm on Facebook here – https://www.facebook.com/issy.brooke – and Twitter here – @IssyBrooke – but as for the million other social media sites, nope. I'd rather be writing…

Thank you for reading.

Issy.

51509204R00185

Made in the USA
San Bernardino, CA
24 July 2017